THE
Marshmallow
GARAGE

THE
Marshmallow
GARAGE

For Connie and Alexander

Nettie Firman

NETTIE
FIRMAN

"Life is 10% what happens to you, and 90% how you respond to it."

Charles Swindoll

"Childhood is the bank at which, later in life, a writer will cash his creative cheques."

Graham Greene

"News is about interesting things that happen to uninteresting people, and uninteresting things that happen to interesting people."

Anon

TABLE OF CONTENTS

THE BIRDS AND THE BEES 1968

The Secret Journal of Lacey Jacqueline Pascoe
May 1968

TRESPASSERS BEWARE!

FRIDAY

O ver this half term, I went to the Marshmallow Garage nearly every day. Mr Bagnall was in the pit underneath a car when I got there this afternoon.

"Hello," I called out.

"Hello, my little friend. How's Lacey?"

"I'm fine, thank you. Mum wants some things from the shop."

"Just a minute. I'll be right with you."

Mr Bagnall got out from under the car and wiped his hands on a dirty rag. His hands, face and boiler-suit were streaked with black grease.

"Mum wants some milk, bacon and a sliced loaf. Also some

bananas and a tub of vanilla ice cream." I gave him my basket.

"Does she now. Well, what Mum wants, Mum gets. Right?"

"Yes, that's right."

"How's Mum?"

"Alright, thank you."

"I tell you what, Lacey. You're a good girl and I've got some new sweets in. Take a look at these monsters." Mr Bagnall took a packet of giant marshmallows from a display next to the sweet counter.

"Have you ever seen such enormous marshmallows?"

"No, but Mum didn't say I could buy any sweets today."

"Well, here – you take them, love, and say they're a present from me for doing Mum's shopping."

I thanked him and ate half the packet on the walk home.

Mum was out when I got back and Vinnie was watching the telly, smoking one of those smelly, fat cigarettes. They weren't like the ones Grandad smoked and seemed to make him dozy and a bit weird.

"Where's Mum?" I asked him.

"Dunno."

Vinnie is Mum's boyfriend and he has horrible red, fat, swollen feet, which are always on show, because he wears open sandals and no socks. Says it lets them breathe. His feet stink of rotting meat. His toe nails are black and yellow. He's a swarthy-looking man with dark stubble on his face, a hairy chest and a big belly. Now Mum's lost her job too. She was a traffic warden, but a woman spat at her and Mum punched her in the face and broke her nose. A nasty girl at school said that Mum and Vinnie are called Foot and Mouth. I think that's some kind of disease that cows get. I never knew my Dad, but have a memory of him playing the drums in the lounge in our old house, or maybe I just imagined it because of the photograph. Mum said he'd died, but sometimes I hear her talking to him on the phone, which is strange. But I don't question it. Best to keep out of their way – especially if they're having one of their rows. Maybe Mum thinks he talks to her from beyond. She can be a bit like that. Shame I haven't got any brothers or sisters, but I have my friend Kim, and Mr Bagnall at the garage, although I was once woken up by Vinnie and Mr Bagnall having an argument outside our front door.

It's May half term, and with my pocket money I've bought a lined book from the Post Office to start a diary. I don't have much to write about, but I like writing stories and Miss Connard said I have a gift. She said on my first report last term that I had good powers of observation. Last year I was one of the winners of a children's essay competition for Cadbury's 'The Story of Chocolate', and I won a selection of chocolate bars in a tin, which I then used as a pencil case. No one else has one like it. I hate my name as girls at school call me 'Lacy Pants', but my knickers don't have lace on them, like Mum's do. I wish I was called Cathy or Wendy. We live in a council house on the edge of Tiptree village and sometimes boys throw stones at our windows from the footpath by the field where the ponies are. Once Mum yelled at them that she would tear off their arms and beat them with the soggy ends, and they ran off. I don't have much to do with boys, though I quite like David Lawson from school, but no one must know about that! His mum teaches science at our school. He has dark, curly hair and once shared his packet of chocolate buttons with me at break. His teeth are very white.

Mum's home and it's fish fingers, peas and beans for tea. And ice cream. We only have ice cream at the weekends, and it's Friday night and I'm now on my half-term for ten days. Nothing's planned, but I'm hoping that Mum will allow Kim to come over and maybe stay the night on the blow-up mattress. Vinnie has fallen asleep on the settee and Mum's nattering on the phone to her friend, Chrissie. They talk a lot and it gets on Vinnie's nerves. I slip out to go and see the ponies after supper and take them some carrots. They're very friendly and I call them after planets – Star, the brown one, is my favourite because he has a white star in the middle of his forehead, but I like them all – Pluto, Sunny, Jupiter and Mars.

Our house looks out over the fields, which is where the footpath is, and other kids and teenagers hang around, smoking and that. We haven't lived here very long. We had to move from Chelmsford, as Mum didn't get on with the neighbours and there was some row about a fence, and they accused Mum of poisoning their dog. Mum's a bit hot-headed, but would never do that, I know.

SATURDAY

Every Saturday morning my pocket money of two shillings is on the kitchen table, plus the money for Vinnie's Sun newspaper, so I set off just after eight on my bike to the newsagent. Mr and Mrs Patel are very nice, but they can't stand whistling. They say it's the noise of the devil. I've been in there when boys started whistling on purpose and they went bonkers. I normally buy a packet of Refreshers, Love Hearts, some Black Jacks and Fruit Salads and a Milky Bar or Parma Violets – if they have them – but today I was thinking about the giant marshmallows, so I only got the paper.

"No sweets today, Lacey?" Mr Patel asked me.

"No, thank you." I didn't want to tell him about the marshmallows as it might sound rude.

Mr Bagnall was having a fuel delivery and talking to the man I've seen in the pony field, who was carrying a can of petrol.

"Hello again, my little friend," he said. "Did you like the marshmallows?"

"They were amazing," I said. "I've brought my pocket money to get some more."

"Glad you enjoyed them. They're a shilling a packet." So I took two.

"This is Mr Fisher, Lacey. He owns the ponies in the fields behind your house." Mr Fisher shook my hand hard. His hands were very rough and dirty, and he had short, grey spiky hair, like a prisoner. He was wearing a long, army-coloured coat, with orange string tied around his waist. The coat nearly touched the ground as he wasn't very tall.

"You like riding, girl?" he asked me.

"I'd love to learn to ride, but Mum says we can't afford it."

"How about you help me take the ponies up to my stables at Holts Farm and I'll give you a riding lesson for free? You can help me out a bit, being as it's half term. I'm going up there now as the girls start arriving for their rides at ten."

"Go on, love. You'll have a lovely time." Mr Bagnall said. "I'll get you a sandwich from the shop for your lunch."

"I'll have to go and ask my Mum."

"You do that, girl", said Mr Fisher, "and I'll see you at the field gate in fifteen minutes. Wear gumboots, mind, as it's muddy after all this rain."

I couldn't believe my luck and cycled back home as fast as my feet would pedal. Mum was having a cigarette and a cup of tea in the back garden and said she couldn't see why not, being as he was a friend of Mr Bagnall's, but I had to be back by six.

Mr Fisher had caught the ponies and put head collars on them and was waiting by the gate when I got there. "We're going to lead them up the road for ten minutes, where my stables are. Alright, girl? You take these two and follow close behind me. Hold on tight to them ropes now and stay on the edge of the road."

Honestly, I thought I was dreaming as I led those ponies and I hoped that someone I knew might see me, as I felt so important.

The stables were rather run-down and rickety, and there was a large, grassy fenced area with a well-worn track around the edge, and also a muddy strip alongside it. Mr Fisher tied the ponies up to the fence and went to get brushes and things to groom them with. He showed me what to do and with what and I got most of the mud out. The ponies seemed to like it.

"Now we do their manes and tails, girl. Be careful when you're behind them and don't go doing anything silly or stupid, or shout, as they might kick you."

I didn't care if they did kick me. It was just the best thing ever, doing that, and I felt dead grown-up and responsible. I followed Mr Fisher into the tack room and he got quite cross.

"No one comes in here, girl. It's private. I keep my gun in here and it's out of bounds to everyone. Understand? See that notice on the door that says 'No Entry'?"

I didn't like the idea of the gun as it sounded dangerous.

"Why do you keep a gun in there?" I asked him.

"That's for shooting rabbits, rats, pigeons and foxes. Alright? Now I'm not here to answer your questions all day, girl. We've got tacking-up to do."

Mr Fisher came out with saddles and bridles and showed me how to tack-up, but it was quite complicated.

"You'll learn," he said.

There was something about Mr Fisher that was a bit odd, sort of shifty. He had small pale blue, darting eyes, like a tropical fish. He looked like a stoat or a weasel, with his small vermin-like face, and wore boots with metal caps on the toes. He seemed rather secretive, and it made me feel uneasy. I suddenly wanted my Mum.

Several girls started to arrive, each with a ten bob note. Mr Fisher took the notes and stuffed them in his coat pocket. Two of the girls were in the form above me at school, but they ignored me. There didn't seem to be a system. Some of the girls walked and trotted around the enclosure, but the others could canter up and down the muddy strip. Mr Fisher would just stop them whenever he wanted and someone else got on. The others just sat around on broken plastic chairs, waiting to take their turn again. It wasn't really a riding lesson, and I couldn't wait for my go, but I didn't dare ask Mr Fisher when it would be my turn. I felt quite sad when I ate my egg sandwich (which was a bit stale), but he might get cross if I left and Mum might not allow me back if I went home upset, so I just smiled at him every time he caught my eye. The girls came and went throughout the day and I just watched and waited.

Later in the afternoon after the girls had all left, I helped Mr Fisher untack the ponies, but I desperately needed a wee.

"Now, girl. You still want that riding lesson?" he asked me.

"Yes, please, but could I use your toilet?"

Mr Fisher laughed. "There's no toilet here, girl, but you can go behind the stables over there. If you need a number two, there's a shovel round at the back. Just dig a hole and bury it."

I had left it too late and by the time I'd found a quiet place I'd wet my pants. It was right embarrassing.

"Had a little accident, did we?" Mr Fisher smirked as he looked at the damp patch down my jeans. "Never mind, girl. You can tell your Mum that you got wet from washing the ponies down. Alright? Let's get on with it then. You stand on that mounting block and I'll give you a leg-up." Mr Fisher put the mounting block next to the white pony, the one I called Jupiter. He had a strange way of helping me up and had one of his hands between my legs, which felt odd.

"What's his name?" I asked.

"I don't give them names, makes it too sentimental when they die."

"Could I ride the brown one?" I asked.

"No. She's old and has done enough work for today. Let's get on with it then."

"I call her 'Star'."

"You can call her what you bleeding like, girl. You talk too much." He adjusted the stirrups.

"Now, sit up straight, grip your knees in and lower your heels. Look straight ahead. That's right. Hold the reins with your little finger outside and not too tight, not too loose. That gives you more control, that does."

Mr Fisher led me around the track. It felt great. After four or five times around, he took off the leading rein and said I could have a go on my own, with him walking beside me.

"Now, you give the pony a little nudge with your heels to walk on. If you want to stop, just pull the reins gently. That's it."

At that moment, I found true happiness. I would make it my life to work with ponies. I walked around on my own for a few more laps and then it was over.

"You've done well, girl. That's enough for today then. Do you want to come again tomorrow?"

"Yes, please."

I helped Mr Fisher give the ponies a brush down and then we walked them back to the field. Mum was frying chips and boiling frankfurters for tea and Vinnie was cleaning his darts. He plays darts every Saturday evening, sometimes with Mr Bagnall, while Mum has drinks at the bar and I play on the swings or do my homework or colouring inside if it's cold or raining. It's good, as I get a Coca-Cola and a packet of crisps, with a little blue bag of salt in it. You have to open the bag of salt carefully and shake it in with the crisps, but they have to last me the whole evening, so I ration myself. I only get Coke at the pub, and I think Mum only gives it to me to keep me quiet.

I rubbed mud into my jeans on the wet patch and Mum told me to put them in a bucket to soak, which was a relief. I started telling her about my day as I laid the table. She seemed pleased I'd had a good time, and I asked her if I could go tomorrow and she said yes.

"Who is this Mr Fisher man anyway?" she asked me.

"He's a friend of Mr Bagnall's and his stables are at Holts Farm, just up the road."

Mr Bagnall called to collect us at half past seven.

"How did you get on today with the riding, Lacey?" he asked me.

"It was brilliant. I rode a pony all by myself. Tomorrow, Mr Fisher said he'll teach me how to trot."

"Well, that's good and will keep you out of mischief, won't it, Lacey? And here's some apples and lettuce for the ponies as they're going a bit soft. I'll probably see you up there tomorrow as it's my day off and Mr Fisher shuts early on a Sunday and we catch rabbits. It's fun."

"Do you catch them with fishing nets?" I asked him.

"You're no fool, are you Lacey? You're quite right, but it's not quite how you think."

"Oh." I liked the idea of catching rabbits.

SUNDAY

After I'd made myself a cheese sandwich, I met Mr Fisher and the ponies by the gate at nine.

"Alright, girl," he said.

"Yes, thank you, but my name's Lacey."

"I know that, but it's not my policy to call girls by their names. Too personal, like."

"I suppose there are a lot of names to remember."

"I know all their names, girl, but don't choose to use them. Alright? Let's get going then."

I led the same ponies and it felt just as good as yesterday.

When we got to the stables, Mr Fisher asked me to get some hay from the lean-to next to the 'Private' tack room. It was very dusty in there and full of cobwebs, but I don't mind spiders. The lean-to was stacked with logs, hay bales and big plastic sacks of carrots, bran, oats and pony nuts, and there was a large plywood tea chest overflowing with moth-eaten, faded velvet hats.

"Fill up them metal buckets with water from the tap, girl, and give the ponies a drink with their hay while you groom them."

It didn't feel as strange as yesterday and I felt quite at home. Mr Fisher seemed to be in a better mood too. He was picking dirt out of the hooves whilst I was grooming them.

"I saw Mr Bagnall last night," I said.

"Oh yes, and what did he have to say?"

"He said I could go with you and catch rabbits when the riding's over today."

"Did he now. You're not squeamish then, girl?"

"No."

"I don't see why not then. We could do with an extra pair of hands with all them rabbits to catch."

I asked him where he kept the rabbits he'd caught and he just laughed. There weren't so many girls today. A few came again, but mostly new ones. The day was much the same, but I knew I would have to wait my turn until they'd all gone. At least I knew where to go and have a wee though.

When all the girls had left, Mr Fisher gave me a leg-up the same way and said I could walk round on my own a few times, then he attached the leading rein.

"Now, we're going to do a little trot, girl. I want you to sit down hard in that saddle, right?" We went half way round the track and then stopped.

"How was that then?" he asked me.

"Not very comfortable."

"That's right. That was a sitting trot and now you have to learn how to do a rising trot, like you've seen those girls do. Off you get now and I'll show you." He untied the lead rein and got on the pony, quick as a flash.

"Go on then," he said, and I watched his rising motion carefully.

"Now, you just go with the rhythm of the pony and rise up and down, like I did. There's only one way to do it, like making babies, and you'll soon learn." He re-attached the leading rein.

"We'll walk a bit and then you ask him to trot on, with your heels."

It was a bit clumsy at first and still not comfortable. I lost one of my stirrups and felt stupid and a bit scared, but he didn't get cross.

"Takes a while to get used to, girl, but you'll get it with practice. Want another try?"

"No, thank you. Maybe tomorrow."

"You're not frightened then?"

"No, but my legs feel a bit shaky."

"Whereabouts?" he asked eagerly.

"At the top."

He started to rub the inside of my legs and then sort of frantically itching himself under his coat. Then he made a little grunt and I dismounted.

"Have you been bitten?" I asked him.

"Yes, them ruddy horse flies, they get everywhere."

We got on with feeding the ponies their nuts and bran from large plastic containers and Mr Fisher gave me an extra strong mint.

"Did you know that ponies love peppermints, girl?"

"No."

"They do, and you can give them one each. Here, but keep your hands flat, mind, else they'll bite your fingers off."

"Do they like Polos?" I asked him.

"They like any mints and can smell them in your pocket, too."

Mr Bagnall arrived in his pick-up truck shortly afterwards.

"Afternoon, Douglas," he said to Mr Fisher. "How did Lacey do today?" He gave me a wink.

"She did well, but the trotting still needs a bit of work."

"Jolly good. All set then?"

Mr Fisher went into the lean-to and came back with several sacks and a handful of what looked like yellow netball nets. We walked past the place where I do my wee and continued up a track until we came to an open, grassy area on a slight mound. The ground was covered with rabbit holes – there must have been twenty or thirty. Mr Fisher and Mr Bagnall got to work covering the holes with the netting and securing them with long metal pins, hammered into the ground. Then Mr Fisher brought out a long white animal from one of the sacks.

"What's that?" I asked.

"This is Jiminy, my ferret. He's going to go down them burrows and flush them rabbits out. You just watch now, and when you see one of them nets moving, you go over and kneel right over the netting so the rabbit can't get out and wait until I come over. Right?"

Mr Fisher released Jiminy and he darted straight down one of the holes. A few minutes later, two of the nets had trapped a rabbit.

"Go, girl, quick. Over there. Terry, you cover the other one." Mr Fisher shouted. The poor creature was writhing around and screaming, like a scalded cat, then Mr Fisher came over and banged it hard on the head with his hammer. Its eyes bulged and honestly, I thought I was going to be sick. Over the next half hour or so, they trapped and killed about fifteen rabbits. There were two babies, but one escaped, and I asked Mr Fisher if I could keep the other one as a pet.

"They don't make pets, girl. They's wild. They's a different breed to the ones you get in a pet shop and usually die within a few days if kept in captivity. This is kinder." The men started to take off the nets and Mr Fisher blew a slim, high-pitched silver whistle. Jiminy appeared out of one of the holes with blood around his mouth. He had little, pink, beady eyes.

"Good lad," said Mr Fisher and stuffed him back in a sack. I think Mr Bagnall saw that I was upset and he put his arm around my shoulder.

"Do you think Mum would like a couple for the pot, Lacey?" he asked me. "Take them anyway and if she doesn't want them you can bring them up to me tomorrow morning and I'll put them in my freezer. Now, you'd better be getting off home as Mr Fisher and I generally have a couple of stouts of a Sunday evening."

"What about walking the ponies back?" I asked.

"They'll be stabled here tonight girl, but if you want to come up again tomorrow, we'll have another lesson at the end of the day. And remember to bring that sack back."

"I don't want to do this again though," I said as I walked off, but I don't think the men heard me. So I made my way home, with the dead rabbits swinging in the sack.

MONDAY

Mum was right disgusted by the dead rabbits I brought home last night, but Vinnie said he'd deal with them.

"It's free food, isn't it, Jacks, and they make a good stew."

Mum wanted him to take the bloody things to the butcher and exchange them for sausages, but Vinnie held his ground and said he would skin and prepare them. Mum told him that she didn't want to come back to a mess in the kitchen or any sign of blood. In the Co-op, she'd seen an advertisement: CASHIERS AND STACKERS NEEDED and wanted the cashier's job; we went along together so I could help her with the shopping.

Mum dolled herself right up and had done her eyelids with black flicks at the corners, like the film stars do, and put on her green, flowery dress and high heels. She always wears trousers and I'd only seen her wear that dress once since we've been here and that was the night Mr Bagnall and Vinnie had the argument. I remember it clearly because she was sobbing at the kitchen table, with her head in her hands, and Vinnie was yelling at her. I saw him give Mum a slap, so I made her a mug of cocoa.

"Good morning," Mum said to a spotty young man at Customer Services in the Co-op in her poshest voice. "Ai've come about the position of Cashier."

"And your name is?"

"Jacqueline Pascoe, Mrs."

The man disappeared through some plastic flaps and came back a few minutes later.

"Mr Barrett, our manager, will see you at three o'clock this afternoon. Please bring along your employment history and any references you have."

"Thank you so much for your help," she purred, fluttering her eyelids.

"Well done, Mum. You've got an interview and you sounded ever-so professional."

"These frigging shoes are killing me, kid," she said. "You get the shopping and I'll wait here. Get yourself a bar of chocolate too. Here's the list."

"Could I get Polos instead?" I asked her.

"Of course, but just get on with it. I need a cigarette and a cuppa."

We had fried eggs on toast for lunch, then I headed off to the stables. It was busy and Mr Fisher didn't see me arrive, so I walked up to the rabbit mound again to watch them hopping about, and went to look at a run-down caravan a bit further down the hill. It seemed to be lived-in. I tried to open the door, but it was locked, so I picked some wild flowers for Mum to pass the time. When I got back to the stables there were a group of girls in a huddle. I'd seen them there on Saturday and I knew they were talking about me by the way they looked.

"Where've you been, madam?" one of them asked.

"To look at the rabbits."

"Awhh, how sweet. Picked some flowers too? They for Mr Fisher?"

The girls laughed and I knew they were making fun of me.

"How comes you don't pay for your riding, then?" the one with frizzy hair and freckles, sucking a lollipop, asked.

"Because Mr Fisher's a friend of a friend, and I help him out instead," I replied.

"A friend of a friend, eh? We do have friends in high places, don't we. La-di-da. I bet it's only because you can't afford them," she continued. "My mum says your mum's right common, common as muck, and we don't need more muck around here, do we? There's enough muck about the place." She had gloves on and picked up a handful of horse poo and threw it at me. It hit my arm.

"And your mum's boyfriend's a lazy slob too. That's what my mum says."

I had to agree with her on that point, but didn't say so.

Instead I said: "If you're so well-off, why aren't you having proper lessons at Miss Brady's stables?"

With that, she picked up another handful of poo and this time it hit me on my neck. I got up and started running for the road.

"Oi," Mr Fisher called out. "What's going on? Come here, Lacey, come back now."

"Lacey, eh? Very posh." said the ginger-haired girl.

I was trying not to cry and Mr Fisher noticed.

"You lot being mean to Lacey?" he asked them.

"Just having a bit of a laugh with her, that's all."

"Pack it in. I won't have behaviour like that here. Understand? One more word from you lot and you'll be banned from coming again. Now get out and wait for your mums outside the gate. Get a move on then, and I don't want to see you or your filthy little gobs here again until the weekend."

"But I've only had one go," the girl with the squint protested.

"That's your hard luck. You can explain to your mums why you can't ride again 'til Saturday." The girls made their way out slowly.

"I wasn't going to come again 'til Saturday anyway," one of the girls called out over her shoulder.

"Don't you give me no lip, girl," shouted Mr Fisher. "You're banned from coming here ever again. Get me? Now, sod off the lot of you."

"We'll get you cleaned up in a few minutes, girl," Mr Fisher said to me. "You fetch one of them plastic containers and a spade and pick up all the horse manure from the manege and the strip. I'm going to close early now."

He told the remaining girls that he wouldn't tolerate nasty chat and that was why. It didn't seem fair to punish the others, but nobody argued with Mr Fisher. I thought it was great how he stuck up for me and was quite surprised. He was always surprising me.

After we'd untacked and fed the ponies, Mr Fisher said he'd get the mud off me. We walked to his caravan and I asked him if he lived there.

"That's right, girl. Nice place I've got here. Nice and cosy. Now I'm going to warm up some water and we'll get you cleaned up. Take your shirt off now and I'll sponge that muck off. Might be best not to tell your mum about this, else she might not want you coming here again. I heard from Mr Bagnall that she's got a temper."

I did as I was told and Mr Fisher produced a pail of water and a slab of dense, dark green soap from a rusty tin. He started to sponge my neck and front and it stank horribly.

"I don't like that smell," I told him. "It smells of tarmac."

"That's right girl. It's antiseptic, and there's no better thing to wash with. Coal tar, that is. Gets rid of all germs – or would you rather smell of horse dung?"

I asked him if he had a bath and he kicked at a tin bath, which was filled with something disgusting – brown and slimey. I didn't know what it was.

"What's in your bath?" I asked him.

"Them's rabbit skins from the ones we caught yesterday. Them's curing for a week in salt and alum. Then I cleans them up and washes them again, before hanging 'em out to dry and they make beautiful, soft pelts. I makes bed covers and the like and they make good money. I sell them at the market. I'll show you one day."

I was still without my shirt and rather strangely Mr Fisher asked if he could take a photograph of me. Said it was a hobby of his, photographing wildlife.

"You look like a mermaid, sitting there, girl" he said. I really didn't mind as I liked the idea of looking like a mermaid.

Although the afternoon had gone without a ride, I wanted to get home, so we walked the ponies back to the field and arranged to meet in the morning at the usual place, usual time.

Mum noticed the smell of the horrible soap as soon as I walked in the door.

"What's that stink, Lacey?"

I told her I'd had to have a wash from the stables' tap as I'd fallen in horse poo.

"Yuk", Mum said. "Take off all your clothes and go and have a bath now."

She seemed in a good mood and said that the interview had gone well and she should hear in a few days.

TUESDAY

Kim came back today from staying with her Nan and Grandad in Lowestoft, so I was looking forward to seeing her and maybe going to the stables together. As I'd run out of marshmallows, I biked to the garage before meeting Mr Fisher. Mr Bagnall was at the pumps.

"How's tricks, Lacey?" he asked me.

"Fine, thank you, but I don't have any money with me, so could I owe you for a bag of marshmallows, please?"

"'Course love. Going riding today? And have you got a sandwich for lunch? Here – take these, and don't worry about the money."

I told him about Mum's interview, which he seemed to know about.

"Between you, me and the gate post, Lacey, I don't think your mum's got the temperament to be a cashier. You can get some difficult customers, and you know what a short fuse she's got on her."

"She's pretty certain she's got the job." I told him.

"We'll see about that. Off you go now and give my best to Mr Fisher."

After the usual grooming, feeding and tacking-up, the girls started arriving and I set about mucking out the stables. It was hard work and I was pleased to have the marshmallows. There was a lull at lunchtime, so Mr Fisher said I could have my lesson then. It went really well and I almost got the hang of the rising trot, but not off the leading rope. I really did enjoy walking round the manege on my own and telling the pony to stop or walk on. What I don't like are the little flaps of grubby foam that stick in my hair from the moth-eaten riding hats. A lot of the girls have their own hats, proper riding boots and yellow gloves.

When it got busy again, I asked Mr Fisher if I could go and pick some flowers for my mum as I'd forgotten the ones from yesterday after the girls were mean to me.

"Them wild flowers don't last long without water, girl. I'll get you a jam jar and some water. I'm glad you like flowers," he said. "If you like I'll show you something special later, when everyone's gone."

"Thank you."

I was starting to like Mr Fisher. He had a kind heart, even though he could be a bit narky and unpredictable. As he was in a good mood, I asked him if I could bring my friend along tomorrow for a riding lesson, and that maybe she could help out, like I do.

"She'd have to pay for riding here, and I don't need no more help, now I've got you. Too many cooks spoil the broth, girl. Know what I mean? We've a good arrangement here, just you and me, like."

I picked ten different kinds of flowers, but some had short stems and some long, so it was a bit tricky to keep them all in the jam jar. I sat and watched the rabbits before making my way back. Mr Fisher was untacking.

"There you are, girl. Everyone's gone now, and once we've fed the ponies, I'll take you up to my caravan to show you what I promised."

He told me to wait outside the caravan and came out with an old-fashioned leather photo album. Inside were hundreds of pressed, dried flowers, and their funny names written alongside in neat, spidery writing.

"Them's names are Latin, girl. There was nothing my Mum didn't know about flowers or herbs. She used to make potions and poultices for all of us kids out of herbs, nettles, crushed leaves and flowers. She could cure any ailment."

On the inside of the album it said 'Ethel Mary Fisher, 1910.'

"Your mother has beautiful handwriting," I said.

"My mother was educated with a governess, girl. She was the old Farmer Platt's sister. She and my dad ran off together, but my dad was a Romany and she chose to take the life of simple living, like we Romanies do."

"What's a Romany?" I enquired.

"There's some folks what call them gypsies. No school or education – just living and learning from the countryside and travelling about."

I asked him if he could read.

"I get by, girl."

As this wasn't a yes or a no, I took it that he couldn't. He said I could look through the album, while he went for a piss. When he was out of sight I quickly went into the caravan, where there were loads of photographs of girls from the stables on a pin-board. One of them was actually doing a wee. His bed was covered with rabbit pelts, sewn together like a quilt, and it smelt musty and sour in there.

"Right ho, girl. Time you were getting back, but if you're ever so careful you can borrow the album and see if you can find them flowers you picked. They'll all be in there in order of the seasons. Give you something to do tomorrow as I'm going to give the ponies a day's rest." He put the album and my flowers in a plastic bag and said he'd see me on Thursday.

"Can I see Jiminy?" I asked him.

"I'll show you Jiminy some other time, and all the other animals I've got. Alright?"

We walked the ponies back to the field and Mum was in a right bait when I got home. The Co-op had said that, in view of her references, she couldn't work as a cashier, but could take a stacker's position. This involved working three nights a week for four hours, when the deliveries came. As we needed the money, she'd accepted the job and would start on Thursday night; the deliveries being on Thursdays, Saturdays and Tuesdays. At least the pay was double for being night work.

"Bleeding cheek," she said, while frying our sausages for tea. "They don't know something good when they see it. Bugger them. No one messes with me, plus I'll miss the Saturday evenings at the pub. They told me it's three nights or nothing."

The dead rabbits were lying on the draining board in the kitchen. They looked bloated.

"Vinnie," Mum yelled. "Get on with dealing with those bloody rabbits or I'm going to throw them away."

Out of curiosity, I watched Vinnie chop their paws off at the joint and nick the skin all the way along their stomachs and around their necks. Then, by holding around their necks, he peeled back the skins and threw them in a bucket before chopping off their heads and pulling out their innards. The smell was terrible, and Mum wasn't having any of it.

"They're off, Vinnie. Chuck 'em out as I'm not going to be bleeding cooking them, I can tell you."

"That's normal, that smell," Vinnie said. "Just the food breaking down from their guts. Once they've been washed, they'll be fine."

"I'm not cooking or eating them," Mum said. "If you want to, that's up to you." He put them back in the fridge.

Mum let me ring Kim to see if she wanted to come over tomorrow and join us to go to Colchester for lunch and see a film to celebrate getting her job. She told Vinnie to make the stew as she wouldn't have the decaying rabbits in the fridge for one more day.

WEDNESDAY

Kim arrived mid-morning and we all took the bus to Colchester. We had loads to talk about, so Mum said we could sit in the back, but we were too busy chatting to wave to the cars behind. Kim had bought us sticks of peppermint rock, with 'Lowestoft' printed all the way through it, so we sucked on our rocks all the way there and still didn't finish them. I told her about the marshmallows and meeting Mr Fisher at the garage. She said she'd once been bitten on the back by a pony and was frightened of them, so didn't want to learn to ride, which was a shame. Then we walked from the bus station to Lyons Cafe in the High Street, where we had lemonades and toasted teacakes. Mum had a coffee and a cigarette. Mum asked Kim about her time away and she said it had been boring, apart from the food.

"We had fish and chips and orange Fanta every day, but Nan and Grandad slept in the afternoons, so me and Danny just watched telly or went to the harbour to see the fishing boats come and go, and unload their nets."

Mum said she wanted to go to the market to buy some new clothes, and she gave us five bob each to spend, so I bought some yellow cotton gloves for riding, and Kim a scarf for her Mum's birthday. We had just enough change for an ice cream. Then Mum took us to the cinema to see 'Jungle Book', while she went to the dentist and did some more shopping. We got a bag of popcorn each and a coke. It was brilliant. I've never known Mum to be so generous, and the film was good too.

Kim said she had to be back by five as it was her mum's birthday and they were having family over for tea, so I walked her back home and was looking forward to identifying my wild flowers with the help of Mr Fisher's album. When I got back, Mum had changed into her new orange mini-dress, crocheted cardigan and black, patent imitation Mary Quant boots. Vinnie had cooked the rabbit stew, which smelled quite nice, but I wasn't sure I fancied it.

"Tastes just like chicken," he said, and gave me a spoonful of the gravy, but I still didn't want it, so Mum and I had spaghetti hoops on toast and watched Crossroads.

"Mr Bagnall's got kittens," Mum told me as we were washing up.

"Please can I have one, Mum. Please, please. I promise to look after it. Can I go and see them now? Please," I begged.

As she was all dolled-up like on a Saturday night, she said

that if it was okay with Mr Bagnall, she could drop me off there for an hour or so while she and Vinnie went to the pub. Mr Bagnall never said no to anything Mum asked him. Vinnie dished up a portion of the stew in an ice cream tub for Mr Bagnall, and also a couple of bottles of his home-made beer, and we made our way round. His front garden was all overgrown with weeds and stacks of wooden pallets, and a rusty old fridge was propped up against the fence. He also had a garden gnome with a fishing rod. I've always wanted a garden gnome, and Mr Bagnall said I could have it. He made me a glass of squash and gave me packet of Twiglets.

"I didn't know Fluffy was pregnant," he told me, "and when I went to bed last night, there she was at the bottom of my bed with six kittens."

"Can I see them?" I asked.

"Come on, then. I've put them in a box in the sitting room, but you can't touch them, as Fluffy wouldn't like that. Of course you can have one! If it's okay with Mum, that is." I told him I'd like the pure white one and would call it Tao, whatever sex it was. I was curious as to how he could tell whether they were boys or girls, and he explained it quite well.

"Going riding tomorrow, Lacey?" he asked me.

"Oh yes, I love the riding but some of the girls there are quite mean. Mr Fisher threw them out on Monday as they threw horse muck at me. Please don't tell Mum."

"I wouldn't stand for that either, but Mr Fisher was good to you, I hope."

"Yes, he was very good and got me cleaned up."

Mum and Vinnie were gone for hours, and by the time they got to Mr Bagnall's I was pretty tired. I think Mum was a bit tipsy and she was all over Mr Bagnall, which was a bit embarrassing.

He told Mum that I wanted a kitten, but Mum just rushed out into the garden and was sick all over the gnome.

"Too many sherbets and spaghetti hoops for supper?" laughed Mr Bagnall, and he drove us home.

THURSDAY

Mum got up really late and said she'd got a bad headache. She said she needed to have a quiet day in view of starting the job that evening, so it suited her fine that I would go to the stables for the day. I showed her Mr Fisher's album, and said that I wanted to make one similar.

"Sounds a nice bloke if he's interested in flowers. I've got an album you can have, as it happens. Unwanted Christmas present." The album was plastic, not leather, but it had thick white, pull-back sticky pages and label strips for the entries. It was perfect.

I thought that Mr Fisher might be cross with me for not being there to help him take the ponies up, so I biked to the stables and explained that Mum hadn't been well and I needed to get back to look after her.

"That's alright, girl. You come up later and we'll have a lesson then."

I told him about the album and said I would return his mum's one today. He nodded.

I found a shilling on the ground outside the stables and went straight to Mr Bagnall's to buy a bag of marshmallows. He was polishing second-hand cars on the forecourt.

"How's Mum today?" he asked.

"Not too bad. She's going to have a quiet day as she starts her new job tonight."

"Wish her well from me, and I'll get that gnome cleaned up for when you next come round. Alright, love?"

I went home and got straight to work with pressing the flowers into the album. They had wilted a bit, but were still recognisable. I wrote my name inside the front cover, like Ethel Mary Fisher: Lacey Jacqueline Pascoe, May 1968. In my best handwriting I wrote, two to a page, the ten specimens I'd picked:

Bugle	Ajuga reptans
White Campion	Silene alba
Periwinkle	Vinca minor
Marsh Marigold	Caltha palustris
Purple Milk Vetch	Astragulas danicus
Common Toadflax	Linaria vulgaris
Speedwell	Veronica austriaca
Lesser Celandine	R. ficaria
Foxgove	Digitalis purpurea
Birds Foot Trefoil	Lotus corniculatus

I made me and Mum tomato soup and toast for lunch, which was all she fancied. Vinnie had gone out on his trail bike with his mates to ride along the sea wall at Goldhanger. As we ate our soup at the kitchen table, I asked Mum if she loved Vinnie.

"Course I do. Why wouldn't I?"

"Because you seem to like Mr Bagnall – at least you did last night."

"Last night I was drunk, love, and you can do silly things when you're drunk, and then regret them."

"Did you regret what you did last night, then Mum?"

"Do you know what, I can't remember what I did, so it doesn't matter."

Obviously, I don't like to trick Mum, but this gave me the perfect opportunity to say that she'd said I could have one of the kittens.

"Did I now? I'll have to discuss it with Vinnie. Now, why don't you go off riding as I'm going back to bed."

I walked up to the stables with the sticky remains of my rock for the ponies. Mr Fisher was quite right: they could smell them immediately and were nuzzling greedily at my pocket. A couple of girls were cantering up and down the strip.

"You got mints in there, girl?" he asked.

I produced the rock and a packet of Polos.

"Keep your palms flat, that's it. As it's quiet, would you like a lesson now?"

I asked him if I could ride Star for a change, and he said yes.

"Not a bad thing to try out a different pony once you've got a bit of confidence, but she's getting on and her movement is different. You'll see."

She was actually more comfortable to ride than Jupiter, as she's got quite a dip in her back and a slower trot. I got the hang of it much better and Mr Fisher asked if I'd like to go out for a short hack on the leading rein when the girls had gone, which I was keen to do.

"Meanwhile you go round and do some poo-picking for me in the manege, and fill up that water trough with the hose."

I gave him the bag with the two albums.

"I've started my own one, but need to pick fresh flowers to press them properly, if you could teach me how."

"That's not difficult, girl. You put them between tissue or toilet roll, individual like, and press them between the pages of a heavy book, with more books on top to weigh them down for a couple of weeks. Get a move on then."

"That's enough now," he called out to the girls.

"Why does she get free riding lessons?" I heard one of them ask him.

"Not that that's any of your business, but she helps me out here – like what she's doing now. Have I ever asked any of you to go picking up poo and get your pretty little hands dirty? Well then, that's your answer. On your bikes now."

Mr Fisher led me along a grassy track at the bottom of the rabbit mound and past his caravan. There was a fenced enclosure of chickens, geese, ducks, a goat and various tatty hutches and runs.

"Is that where you keep Jiminy?" I asked him.

"That's right. And Elvis, my other ferret. He's black."

"Why do you give Jiminy and Elvis names, and not the other animals?"

"Because I've trained them to catch rabbits for me, and they need to know their names and to obey the command of my whistle. Maybe I'll show you the animals over the weekend, depending on how busy we are. Now, would you like a little trot?"

It felt a bit frightening to be out of the menage, but Mr Fisher ran along beside me until I asked him to stop as I was getting out of breath.

"You see that big mound of freshly-dug earth there, girl? That's a badger sett. Bigger than a rabbit hole and you never see them as theys come out at night, but I leave scraps of food for them most evenings. They'll eat anything – rabbit guts, rotting vegetables and the like."

"You teach me so much, Mr Fisher. My mum likes the idea of that."

"I'll teach you something else, if you want," he said, his eyes brightening. "I'll teach you about the birds and the bees if you like."

"Yes please," I said.

"Well, get off the pony then, and I'll show you."

I dismounted, and Star grazed on the grass.

"Now," he said, "sit down. You know what grown up men and women want? The man wants this...." he pointed to the zip on his trousers. ".... into that, on a lady." He pointed to the place where my wee comes from. "Did you know that, girl?"

"No, I didn't, but Mr Bagnall's explained how he tells the sex of his kittens."

"Now I've told you, it has to be our little secret, alright? You said you wanted me to teach you things, and I've plenty to teach you. That's if you want to learn."

"I do," I said, although truthfully I didn't know what to say and felt a bit uncomfortable. So I said that I had to get back to help Mum with the tea as she was starting her new job tonight.

We walked the ponies back to the field and Mum was in a terrible bait when I walked in.

"Right, Lacey. Sit down in the lounge. You haven't been straightforward with me about everything that goes on at the stables, have you?"

I immediately felt guilty and that somehow, she knew about what Mr Fisher had just told me.

"What do you mean, Mum?" I asked her.

"Mr Bagnall said that you'd told him last night some girls up there were being mean to you. Yes?"

"Yes, Mum, but I didn't want to worry you. It was nothing." I felt betrayed by Mr Bagnall for telling Mum.

"That's not nothing in my book, Lacey. No one bullies my

baby, so I'll be going up to the stables on Saturday to give those girls a piece of my mind."

"Please, Mum, no, don't do that," I begged her. "It would only make things worse, and Mr Fisher wouldn't like any trouble. I might not be allowed up there again if you make a fuss. I won't have the kitten, if that makes a difference."

"We'll see about that. Tea's ready now."

FRIDAY

Grown-ups are always surprising me. They make the rules, then they change them, and I just have to fit in. For instance: I don't know why Vinnie was standing over my bed for such a long time last night, when Mum had gone to work. I wasn't asleep, but I pretended to be. I'd been thinking about my chat with Mr Fisher, but knew it had to remain strictly private, like he said, although I would have liked to discuss it with Kim.

Vinnie made us boiled eggs and soldiers for breakfast as Mum was still asleep. I asked him if he minded about me getting a kitten.

"Kittens grow into cats, Lacey. And they live a long time and need feeding and vets bills and so on. It's a big commitment to get an animal, and I don't think Mum's that keen."

"Okay," I said. I told him of my plans for the day, to take the ponies up and then go to see Kim to do our homework together, and then return to the stables later. He said that would be fine and he'd let Mum know of my whereabouts.

Kim and I went to the library late morning. I got *Swallows and Amazons* out, and *The Mitchell Beazley Pocket Guide to Wild Flowers*, and Kim a book of Asterix cartoons and an Enid Blyton. She loves Enid Blyton. Our English homework was spelling, and to write a two-page story about the best bit of our half term, which was easy for me. Our maths homework was long division. As I was good at English, and Kim good at maths, we helped each other out. Kim's dad works as a warehouse manager at Wilkins Jams, and we had crumpets with jam for lunch. Afterwards, I popped back home.

Mum was still in her dressing gown, and I asked her how the new job had gone last night. She said it'd been hard work, but the men carried the heavy stuff – bottles, tins, cans and the like while the women took the bread, fruit, veg, cakes, crisps and so on. They stacked the shelves and put the rest in the depot at the back. She said it wasn't too bad, but she was tired.

Then I went to the stables. It was busy, so I asked Mr Fisher if I could go and look at the animals and pick some more wild flowers to press.

"Don't you go opening any of them pens now, will you, girl?" he said. I promised not to and he told me to be back in an hour for feeding the ponies and my lesson.

This time I rode the Palomino pony, who I called Sunny. She was young and fast and I felt a bit nervous, but I did have a trot on the leading rein and Mr Fisher said I'd done well, but I would have preferred to have ridden Star.

"You didn't tell no one about what I told you yesterday, did you, girl?" Mr Fisher asked me as we were walking round the manege.

"Of course not, but I did tell Mr Bagnall about the nasty girls and that he'd told Mum. My mum's got a temper on her, but I begged her not to come round over the weekend," I tried to reassure him.

"I don't want no trouble here, girl. Any sign of trouble and you'll be right out. Understand? I don't know why Mr Bagnall told your mum, but you shouldn't have told him. That don't please me."

I felt I was in heaps of trouble and would never understand grown-ups. I tried not to cry, so Mr Fisher said he would teach me how to clean tack to take my mind off things, and we got on with it. I told him about the kitten I might be getting.

"Don't talk to me about cats, girl. I hate cats. They kill the birds and wildlife. Horrid creatures."

"But your ferrets catch rabbits," I said.

"Rabbits need culling, girl. They's pests and eat the crops and multiply like you wouldn't believe. They's different. Plus, you can put them in the pot and use their fur for making things. Rabbit fur is soft and warm."

"I saw you have a tractor by the animals."

"That's right."

"Could I have a go on it with you?"

"Don't see why not, girl, but that's only got one seat so you'd have to sit on my lap."

"Why do you help Farmer Platt so much?" I wanted to know.

"Because he lets me live here in my caravan and keep the ponies, and in return I do jobs for him – ploughing and that, and a bit of game keeping. We're related through my mother as cousins, though he probably wishes we weren't."

I told Mr Fisher that I'd better be going home, so we fed the ponies and walked them back to the field.

Mum and Vinnie were having the biggest row ever when I got back. I gathered Mum didn't get home 'til four in the morning and Vinnie had just rung the Co-op to ask why she'd had to work overtime. Mr Barrett told him that she'd checked out at one thirty at the end of her shift.

"I know where you bleeding were, you whore," he said to Mum. "I'm not an idiot."

"Well you can fucking leave now, I've had it up to here with you." Mum screamed back, but Vinnie didn't respond. Mum told him to get out, not to come back, and kicked him in the shins. Vinnie went to the front door and slammed it hard behind him.

"Men," Mum said. "Don't ever get involved with them."

While I was having supper, I heard her ringing Mr Bagnall, who came round shortly after with a packet of marshmallows for me. Mum told me to go to bed.

SATURDAY

Mum had left a note for me on the kitchen table, saying not to disturb her and that there was no need to get the paper, but she'd left my pocket money out and some cereal for breakfast. I still went to the newsagent to buy a blank exercise book for my flower notes, drawings and private observations. Then I realised I hadn't got any lunch, so went back home to make a sandwich and leave a note for Mum. By the time I got to the field, Mr Fisher had gone.

"Fat load of bleeding help you've been this morning, girl," he said. "I waited for you and I don't like being kept waiting." I said sorry and we groomed the ponies in silence. I just hoped that the horrid girls wouldn't come up – or my Mum – and luckily neither did. While we were tacking up, I asked him if we could still go and see the animals and have a go on the tractor later.

"We'll have to see about that," he said.

"I've bought myself a book for making flower notes and drawings," I told him, hoping to get in his good books again.

"If you want to see the animals later you can help me out with some fence painting today, alright?"

He went into the tack room and came out with some old rags, gloves, and a weeping tin of sticky, black paint.

"Now, you wipe down the fence with them rags to get them cobwebs off, then you paint the creosote on – not too thin, not too thick. Like this."

The paint smelled horrible, like his soap, and the job took me all day. I wondered where Vinnie had gone to, and also who would babysit me tonight when Mum went to work. Maybe Mr Bagnall would.

I was so tired by the time everyone had gone and didn't feel like a riding lesson.

"Come on then, girl. I'll show you my animals, seeing as you've done a good day's work." Mr Fisher said. He took me round the pens and explained that some of the broody bantams were hatching out pheasants' eggs. I asked him why.

"I find them eggs in nests in the hedgerows and take them away for the chickens to raise. Pheasants make bad mothers. Then they grow here for two months and I release them into safe hides in the wood with other young pullets what Farmer Platt buys before they're fully grown. They's released when the shooting season starts in September. You see that I keep Jiminy and Elvis in separate runs. That's because they'd fight, being as they are both hobs. Hobs are the males and jills the females, but I don't keep jills as they're too much trouble, like women are. The hobs are more obedient and they make better hunters too."

"Why do people go shooting?" I asked him.

"That's an expensive sport, that is, for rich town folk who think they're countrymen. They wouldn't know a pigeon from a parrot – or a pork pie for that matter," he ranted. "All dressed up in their fancy gear. Don't get me started on them, girl, but it makes Farmer Platt good money."

There was a clothes line attached to two trees with all manner of dead creatures dangling from it, ranging from a fresh magpie and decomposing squirrels to a beak on a string. It was disgusting.

"Why do you have all those dead birds and squirrels hanging there?" I asked him.

"That's a gibbet, girl. That warns off the other birds and vermin, that does. Every game-keeper has a gibbet, and has done for centuries."

I asked him if I could see inside his caravan, but he said it was private.

"What do you eat? Mr Fisher?"

"I do well, girl. I get fish and chips from Pete's Plaice every Friday night, and Mr Bagnall gives me out-of-date milk, bread, fruit and vegetables from his shop. Sometimes I lights a fire and roast a rabbit or sausages. I get eggs from the chickens, and eat them when they stop laying. In the autumn I pick wild apples and blackberries and make jam on my calor gas stove." It sounded romantic.

I'd been bitten by an insect on the palm of my hand, and it was getting itchy and swollen.

"Have you any Germolene?" I asked Mr Fisher.

"What would I want with Germolene, girl? You need to rub

some plantain leaves on that." He picked up a scrubby kind of thick-leaved weed from the path and crushed it in his hands, before rubbing it on to mine.

Then he showed me his traps for catching stoats and weasels and explained that they get into the pens through the mesh to kill the chickens and eat their eggs. It was fascinating and would give me lots to write about in my new journal. I asked him if he had a girlfriend, but he said he didn't have all day to answer my questions. As it was getting late, he said we'd have to do the tractor ride tomorrow.

I was very surprised to see Vinnie at home, having a beer in the garden with Mum, but didn't ask any questions. Mum said that as Mr Bagnall was playing in the darts final, Vinnie would be babysitting me. I asked her about going to her job, but she said they could fuck themselves – she wasn't born to be a stacker of food in a supermarket. But she would go for just one more shift tonight before finally making up her mind whether to give in her notice or not.

I have a very good sense of smell, and could smell Vinnie's stinky cigarettes while I was doing the washing up. He came into my bedroom after I'd been in bed a while and his feet smelt worse than ever – like the rotting rabbits. He told me that Mum had asked him to look after me extremely well and that we could play a little game. He asked me to lift up my nightie, before he started touching me and scratching himself, with his hand down his trousers, like Mr Fisher had done. It seemed a strange sort of game, and not that much fun.

I told him that I knew about the birds and the bees, as Mr Fisher had told me. And that I knew about the scratching because I'd seen Mr Fisher do it too, and it was because of horse flies.

I told him that you had to rub the wild plant, plantain (P. media) on it.

Vinnie went mad.

"That's not his job. That's my job, or your mum's. You're a weird little girl and a goody-goody, and you've not got the spice of your mum. You'll never find a nice man to take care of you. I'll go over and sort him out tomorrow, that bastard."

"If you go and see Mr Fisher I'll tell Mum about this," I said, and punched him in that place, where Mr Fisher had told me that man wants woman. He said I was a little so-and-so. Except it wasn't so-and-so he called me – it was some word that sounded like cunning. Then I heard the front door slam and knew I would be on my own until Mum returned.

SUNDAY

I met Mr Fisher at the gate and we walked the ponies up and got them fed and groomed. Mr Fisher ran his hand under a rotting window ledge in the tack room and produced a chrysalis in the palm of his hand.

"See this chrysalis, girl? It's very dark and nearly ready to hatch out. It's almost transparent, see? If you like, you can take it home and keep it in your bedroom in a cool place, but when it hatches out you must let it free. It will turn in to a beautiful butterfly, just like you will one day."

And we got on with the day's work, like usual, and the tractor ride was promised later on account of all my help at the stables over half term.

LITTER 2020

I've always detested litter: it's been the bugbear of my life and constantly on my mind. I see it wherever I go and I find it offensive. It all started when I was a boy, and I used to go with my father to litter-pick in the 1970s. Litter wasn't such a concern then as it is now. We lived in a semi-detached, pebble-dash house in Mustow Street, close to the Abbey Gardens, and where I still live. There was a lot of litter in those days, but we donned rubber gloves and filled a black bin bag each: cans, sweet wrappers, crisp bags mainly, we even found used condoms. Not that I knew what condoms were back then, but my father said it was wise to wear gloves. Now we're more aware about polluting the environment with plastic, which is a good thing. My Dad was advanced in his thinking.

* * *

Driving back from the plant stall in Denston, I saw that black bag of rubbish was still on the roadside a few miles south of Bury-St-Edmunds on the A143. I'd seen it there for a couple of weeks. It'd just been dumped, nowhere near a house, and I was surprised the bin men hadn't picked it up. The tip is now shut and the garden waste collection suspended, but general rubbish and recycling are still collected weekly.

The lazy so-and-so's, I thought. Have they no pride in their job?

I always have gloves in my car, so decided to deal with it myself. It was double-bagged, soft, heavy and oozing sawdust, which suggested it may have been chucked out of a car. I slung the bag in the back of my van.

Only last week, when I was taking my elderly neighbour, Edna, for an urgent doctor's appointment, I saw a lady drop something. From a distance I thought it was a dummy, as she was pushing a pushchair.

"Dropped a dummy?" I asked her. She said she hadn't.

On closer inspection, I saw it was a Wispa packet. I couldn't believe how she could just blatantly drop it when there was a bin, not five yards away. I decided not to pick it up for fear of the Coronavirus, so it remained there, in the otherwise un-littered and empty pedestrian precinct. It was on my mind though, all afternoon. I don't wear gloves or a mask in the current circumstances, as my late mother worked as a cleaner in public health and she always said that a peck of dirt does you good. I've got away with it so far. People are taking all this far too seriously, in my opinion – washing everything bought from the supermarket, from tins to toothpaste, in hot, soapy water. I don't do that. A different matter if you're buying loose fruit or vegetables from the market, which had surely been fingered many times, but the market in Bury had been closed for over a month.

Now I have more time on my hands to litter-pick, but as there are so few people about there isn't that much, which is ironic. I've got myself a bit of a name around here for being a do-gooder, but I'm a glorified plumber by trade, like my Dad. I've always been a bit of a loner, and I think people are suspicious of me due to my weak chin and being rather overweight. A customer once likened me to Princess Diana's one and only Private Secretary and Chief of Staff: Patrick Jephson. He resigned in 1996, after her famous Panorama interview.

I fit water softeners and boiling water taps, which are popular and a good earner, but as I'm self-employed I don't qualify for being furloughed. The rules seem a bit unclear, but I might be able to claim a government payment in June. Fortunately, I have enough money, not having a family. Mostly, I feel sorry for those poor people in high-rises, without a garden or a balcony, and with screaming children to self-educate – and maybe an abusive partner.

I've a bit of a fondness for beer and whisky, so it's just as well that the offy is still open. I heard on the news that the sales of booze are up by thirty-one percent, but presumably that's because no pubs, bars or restaurants are open in these strange times. I don't mind the lockdown as things are pretty much the same in my day-to-day life. I don't socialise much, but have always been pleased to help my neighbours with shopping and errands, like my mother did. I mainly eat ready-meals, and sandwiches or a pie for lunch, so it's all pretty easy.

As the garden centres are closed, I get my plants from a roadside stall, half-way between Bury-St-Edmunds and Haverhill. They're good value and I tend to my pots at this time of year – mostly with red and white geraniums and mixed begonias. Although an organised person by nature, my house and garden have never been so well-tended: doorstep scrubbed, fences painted, windows cleaned, paving slabs hosed down and no weeds in my small garden, which consists mainly of planted pots, anyway.

Like my garden, I keep my van in pretty spick and span order, and it had been bothering me that there was still some sawdust to be swept up from the leaking black bin bag. This is a hazard of being a litter-picker. But I tolerate it.

I learnt my trade from my father, who learnt it from his, but now full plumbing qualifications are necessary to practise. I did my four-year apprenticeship with Dad, then one year's experience as a Journeyman before qualifying as a Master Plumber, having passed the Licensing exam. My sister was also part of the family business, doing the accounts, before getting married and moving up north. So, it's not the same as it was, but then nothing is. My van has recently been up-graded and the logo now advertises 'Wm. Pooley and Son, Bespoke Plumbers. Water Softeners and Sparkling Systems to meet your every need. We provide you with the ultimate water-drinking experience.'

I had to re-word the logo to include the Sparkling Systems as there's now a huge demand for the one tap that does it all: filtered, boiling, chilled and sparkling water. I don't hold with them myself as I think, in fact I know, they can be dangerous if not used properly. The early models spat and splattered, causing burns, but they're a good earner and you can pay from four hundred pounds to over four thousand for the most sophisticated ones – such as being able to adjust the level of sparkling to suit your taste. Can you imagine?

I think this Coronavirus business will bring us all back down to earth. Instead of being concerned about the level of fizziness in our water, we should be remembering those Third World countries, which have little or no clean running water, with many relying on filthy wells. In the poorer parts of Egypt they drink from the Nile, which is full of detritus and dead donkeys. It's possible that my love of pure water has something to do with my hatred of litter.

The history of plumbing is quite fascinating and has its origins in ancient Rome, where their taps worked with a similar mechanism to the ball valves used today. The modern all-singing, all-dancing taps represent the pinnacle of this endeavour, signifying ease, comfort and cleanliness; a brainwave, born in 1970 by Dutch-born Henri Peteri, who worked for Unilever. Whilst attending a presentation about instant soup, it occurred to him that it couldn't be 'instant' if you had to wait for a kettle to boil. So the idea was formed. Pure Brilliance. The word 'plumber' also dates from the Roman Empire as the Latin word for lead is 'plumbum', which amuses me. I sometimes explain this to my customers, but they never seem to be that interested.

* * *

It's Friday and V.E. Day, but what makes it significant is that an ambulance is parked outside my front door at nine thirty a.m. Edna has been feeling poorly for the past few days and is now being carried into the ambulance on a stretcher by paramedics. It seems that her carer is worried she may have the Coronavirus, as she's gone downhill rapidly since yesterday. She's asked me if I'd be prepared to look after Winston, Edna's pug, as she lives in a flat on the fourth floor, and can't care for him.

As I help Edna out with shopping and walking Winston, I have a key to her house, so I know where everything is for him. He's also getting on and all he really needs is a trot around the block to sniff at lamp posts and other dogs' business. I don't like poo-picking – that really is disgusting – but he isn't a bad little fella, despite his appallingly bad breath.

Down my street, preparations were being made for a safe-distancing party, which I won't be attending, as I'm not one for social gatherings. Normally, I would have gone to see my Dad in his care home this morning as we would have enjoyed watching the seventy-fifth celebrations of V.E. Day today together, but visiting hasn't been allowed for a few weeks now. Not that Dad always knows if I'm there as he has Alzheimer's, but it makes me feel better. He was born in 1945 and can remember his post-war childhood vividly. Today, there's Union Jack bunting up in people's front gardens and someone's playing the Last Post on a trumpet, which is moving, and it's a beautiful, sunny day.

Clips of Winston Churchill's Victory Speeches and all the street celebrations of 1945 were on the telly all day, and I thought it was quite a coincidence that I now had my own Winston to look after. They say that plumbers have a lot of coincidences, and I do find it so – although mainly things happen to me in twos, not threes. I might not have fitted a water softener for a couple of months and then get two orders for identical units on the same day, or a request to install two new taps in the same street within a week.

It seemed a shame to be indoors, so I took a cold can of Special Brew out to my greenhouse to transfer the tomato, bean and cucumber plants into Gro-Bags. Then I got my tool box and the bag of rubbish out of the van and sorted out all the washers, screws, nuts, rings and so on into graded compartments, and washed out the dusty plastic container. It was a satisfying job, and one that needed doing, although I had no idea when work would start again. After walking Winston round the block, I fed him and rang the hospital. Edna was in intensive care and it didn't sound good. As she'd lost her husband many years ago, and her only daughter had died in a car accident, there was no one to inform. We were kind of in the same boat – me, Edna and Winston. After a few more beers, curiosity got the better of me and I retrieved the black bag and its mysterious contents from the dustbin.

I laid out a clean dust sheet on the paving and emptied it out. Nestled amongst the sawdust were some very small, fragile white bones - possibly from a cat or a rabbit. Biology, bones and skeletons are not my strongest point, but I sorted them as best I could and graded them by size, like the washers, nuts and screws, carefully brushing off the sawdust. The fact they'd been dumped in the middle of nowhere made me suspicious, and the fearful thought they might be human remains crossed my mind. In case a visiting fox, or indeed Winston, should investigate the bones, I carefully wrapped them in kitchen roll and then put them into an empty biscuit tin. It occurred to me that I should perhaps ring the police, but after a quarter of a bottle of Scotch and several beers I decided it was best to wait until the morning.

* * *

Winston was barking for his breakfast earlier than I would normally have got up, but I indulged him, in case he was missing Edna and his familiar surroundings. After a good fry-up, I rang the police and was put through to Detective-Superintendent Mayhew by the duty officer, due to the 'nature of my call'.

"And why exactly did you pick up this bag, sir?" he asked me. "Most people wouldn't do that sort of thing."

I told him I was fanatical about litter and fly-tipping.

"I see," he said curtly. "I think we'd better pay you a visit this morning and remove your findings. I take it you'll be at home. Your address then, sir?"

Already the tone of the conversation made me uneasy, and I felt I was under suspicion.

Superintendent Mayhew and a lady P.C. got to me around midday, examined the bones with gloves, and said they didn't think they were from an animal.

"And would you be able to take us to the exact spot where you found the bag, sir?"

"Of course, Officer. I pick up litter in Abbey Gardens and on the streets, and I'm known to the Park Wardens," I told him, trying to ingratiate myself. "I hate litter, and now I've the time to deal with it."

"Seems a strange sort of pastime, Mr Pooley, collecting other people's rubbish." Mayhew said dryly as he put the biscuit tin and sawdust into separate dark green police bags, marked 'FORENSIC', with a case number, and taped them shut. "And why did you feel it necessary to look into the bag, sir? I take it you didn't wear gloves to handle these bones?"

"No, I didn't know what I was going to find, did I? I was curious as to why someone would want to dump a bag of sawdust, and surely sawdust would eliminate fingerprints anyway?" Mayhew ignored my comment.

"We'd better be getting along then, sir, so you can show us exactly where you found the bag. No need to take your vehicle, we'll bring you back."

I hate the manner the police speak in this patronising way. It's always 'vehicle', not 'car', and they have a knack by this way of talking of making you feel like a suspect or a simpleton.

We set off, me in the back. Lots of calls came through on their radio and they chatted amicably on the fifteen-minute journey.

"We're close now, Officer," I said, "about fifty yards on the left. Yes, just here." He stopped the car.

"You're quite sure this is the precise location, sir?" the P.C. asked me.

"Quite certain. A hundred percent. Slightly in the ditch it was. You can still see some sawdust there."

"And what was the purpose of your travelling along this road on Thursday?" she continued. This really made me nervous as it was technically an unnecessary journey, and I could be fined for not travelling to get food, medical supplies or emergencies, but I needed to be truthful.

"I was on my way back from buying plants from the roadside stall in Denston. That can easily be verified." Fortunately, the unnecessary travelling bit wasn't picked up on.

They got out of the car and the P.C. took some photographs on her phone before hammering steel rods in to the verge and taping them together with striped Police tape.

"We'll be making some local enquiries, sir, but we'll get you home now and you'll be hearing from us shortly."

I fancied a pie for a late lunch and needed to get the paper, so walked with Winston to the local Co-op. It was such a hot day that some Chinese people in the safe-distance queue had umbrellas up. After queuing for twenty minutes, I needed a cold beer, so bought a four-pack from the chiller, and had my pie and a couple of beers on a bench marked 'Strictly One Person Only' outside the Almshouses. It was all so unreal – nobody about on the streets – and the uncomfortable, recurring thought that my good deed had somehow got me into deep water. I read the Express in the garden and then went inside to binge-watch 'The Office' box set. I'd seen it many times before, but it appeals to me as I've never worked in an office environment, being a sole-trader, and I liked the camaraderie. I would probably have made friends if things had been different, but I've a few old biddies in my street, who I help out, and more often than not they invite me in for a cup of tea to regale me with their ailments.

After lunch I went in to Edna's to check everything was turned off, and to water her garden. As she has no living relatives, and in view of our long family association, I was one of her executors. Although her house was council-owned, I knew she'd left everything to me. I rang the hospital to be told she was on a ventilator and her life was in the balance.

The day and the heat, plus having consumed several beers, made me feel heady, so I only felt like beans on toast, around six. Then I walked Winston round the block, and was quite pleased to do so. Should Edna not make it, many tradesmen have a dog in their van for company, so I'd be quite happy to keep him. I'd recorded all yesterday's V.E. programmes, but the good atmosphere was now gone and I regretted not making more of it. Winston and I were on the settee watching telly when the telephone interrupted us. I feared it would be the police, but it was the manageress of Dad's home to inform me that he had a temperature and that his breathing was laboured.

"Do you think he may have Coronavirus?" I asked her.

"It's possible, but we've no cases here. None of our residents have left their rooms for the past three weeks now, as you know, and our hygiene policies are very rigorous. The staff are now living-in and we're only open for deliveries."

She told me she'd called an ambulance, and I reminded her that I held a signed document, done in the early stages of his Alzheimer's, confirming he didn't want to be resuscitated.

"That's as well you told me, Mr Pooley, I'd forgotten that. I'll inform the ambulance crew."

The second co-incidence in two days, and not a good one,

with both Edna and Dad within yards of each other in West Suffolk Hospital.

Out of interest, I googled local litter-picking jobs, but the ones advertised didn't appeal, as I did that anyway. What did appeal were the motorway pickers, who wore high-viz jackets, as those people really did make a difference. But the pay was low at between nine and ten pounds an hour. What a day. Winston and I went to bed.

The phone was ringing when we got back from our morning walk, and I knew it would be bad news either way. It was the police, and they wanted me at the station right away. I put on my one and only suit, which was a little tight, and a Paisley tie, in need of dry cleaning. Despite the urgency of the call, I was kept waiting on a hard plastic chair for ages before an officer appeared, not Mayhew, with a notepad, buff file and a recording machine. I followed him in to an interview room, and the lady P.C. from yesterday joined us.

"Thank you for helping us with our enquiries, Mr Pooley. I'm Detective Chief Superintendent Paul Willis, and I believe you've met my colleague, P.C. Hutton. This interview is now going to be recorded." He gave the date, time and name of those present, before continuing, "I understand that you're a plumber by trade, Mr Pooley. Is that correct?"

"Yes, that's correct. I'm fully qualified and can provide references."

"And in the course of your work, have you ever found human bones in a blocked drain?"

"Never," I replied, "but my father did on several occasions. He was more of a general plumber than I am. I mainly fit water softeners and kitchen taps."

"So you wouldn't say you have an interest in osteology then?"

"Osti – what?" I asked.

"Osteology – the study of bones."

"Absolutely not."

"But I understand you do have an interest in litter-picking, Mr Pooley."

"That's right. I can't abide litter – it's a bit of an obsession for me."

"So, are you in the habit of picking up other people's bin bags from the roadside?"

"Actually, I've never done it before," I admitted.

"Mr Pooley. We've called on properties within a two-mile radius of the finding of the black bag on the A143 and no one has recalled seeing that bag before."

"That may be because my van is higher than cars and has better vision, as the bag was partially in the ditch. Maybe people aren't so observant as I am, and why would I invent this? Surely, it's my right to get legal assistance? You're treating me like a suspect."

"Mr Pooley, this is an initial fact-finding interview. You're not being accused of anything and you don't need legal assistance at this stage. Let's continue, shall we?" There was a pause.

"Having picked up the bag, why did you find it necessary to look inside it?"

"I was curious, officer, as sawdust was leaking out and I wondered why someone would want to dump a bag of sawdust."

"Our station's forensic officer was on duty over the weekend and he's confirmed that the bones are that of a premature baby, probably some forty years old. Bones of a baby are mostly made up of cartilage, which disintegrates quickly, so they don't have the density of mature bones. Have you anything to say?"

"I'm very sorry to hear that, officer, but I've nothing to add to what's been said. As I told you, I just picked up the bag, as a good deed, and put it in my van. I shouldn't have looked inside, and wish to God I hadn't. Can I go home now?"

"And how long have you lived in Mustow Street, sir?"

"All my life. It was an ex-council house and my father bought it in the 1990s."

"I see. And were you in a relationship around forty years ago?"

"No," I replied. "I've lived with my parents all my life, like I said, and never married."

"Right. This interview will be terminated shortly, Mr Pooley, but as you're our only contact on this case we'll need to undertake a full search of your property and garden. We're just doing our job, as I'm sure you'll understand. We'll be visiting you early this afternoon, if that's convenient. I'm going to terminate this interview now at 10.49 hours, pending further investigations." He gave me a case number.

The stress of it all brought me out in a sweat: I sweat easily. The P.C. poured me a glass of water, and I was shown the door.

When I got home, I cried. I seldom cry, and haven't done so since seeing my late mother lowered into her grave, six years ago. Dad's been going downhill ever since. In view of the pending police visit, I resisted the temptation to down several beers, but had some alcohol-free ones, which almost hit the spot, but not quite. D.S. Willis and P.C. Hutton arrived a couple of hours later and proceeded to search my 'premises', but as I've nothing to hide I wasn't worried. It was invasive though, so I sat in the garden with a cup of tea, where they joined me after also searching my greenhouse.

"Your garden's recently been paved, sir?" Willis asked me accusingly.

"Yes. I did it myself last year."

"And can you account for this bag of sawdust in your greenhouse?"

"Yes. It's walnut sawdust and a natural weedkiller. You sweep it between the cracks and it keeps the weeds away, or mix it with manure or a nitrogen supplement and it keeps plants healthy and moist. Walnut composition is mainly cellulose, and is an organic compound, insoluble in water."

"Chemistry our strong subject, is it then sir?" he said sarcastically. "I've never heard that before, but I do happen to know that cedar sawdust, mixed with zinc sulphate, is a natural preservative, and has been used for centuries as an embalming process. Were you aware of that fact?"

"No," I answered honestly, "H_2O is my strong subject." I congratulated myself on my rather witty reply.

"And have you got proof of purchase of this sawdust, sir?"

"Possibly. I'll look."

"We'll be putting an article in the Bury Free Press next week, appealing for information, and to see if there are any leads on this case. Details will be given about the findings of the bag, but you won't be mentioned by name."

"Thank you."

Willis told me that the sawdust would be examined, and compared to the contents of the black bag. I said that was fine with me as sawdust is easily identifiable – oak, cedar, walnut, pine, etc. They took the bag and left, with the promise of being in touch soon. After a large Scotch, I took Winston round the block to clear my head.

Just as I was getting ready for bed, I got a call from the

hospital to say that Edna had passed away from kidney failure and Coronavirus. I felt gutted. It would be down to me to arrange her funeral, which, due to the lockdown, would be a meagre, poorly-attended cremation, with only me and her carers allowed as mourners.

This prompted me to enquire about my Dad's health, and I was advised that he was on a ventilator and at a critical point.

* * *

I couldn't register Edna's death on Monday as it was a Bank Holiday, but did so over the phone on Tuesday, and also informed Social Services and the Council. I appointed a funeral director, the same one who'd done my Mum's. Then I went into Edna's house to turn off every appliance and look for legal documents so that I could inform her solicitor, who I knew was the joint executor. Edna didn't have many possessions apart from a lot of china pug ornaments, crocheted blankets and soft toys. She had kept her house neat and tidy, and it was easy enough to find the paperwork in her teak desk – bank statements, her will, Premium Bonds and savings books. She had two thousand pounds of Premium Bonds and just under four thousand in her bank account, which would easily cover the funeral costs. Her will was in a sealed envelope, which I decided to leave to open with the solicitor.

All her furniture was tired and destined for the tip, when it re-opened, and any other useable chattels would have to go to a charity shop in due course. I spent a couple of hours bagging up her clothes and putting crockery, cutlery and paintings into boxes. I found two hundred pounds in a teapot, which I pocketed to put towards costs for Winston. This didn't feel dishonest, as I was sure that Edna would have wanted the money to go towards his upkeep.

As it happened, Winston had taken to 'scooting', which I'd never heard of. He crouched down and dragged his rear end along the ground, as if to itch it. I knew where his vet was, since for the past couple of years, I'd taken him, and Edna, for his annual vaccinations and nail-clipping. So I gave them a call. I spoke to a nurse, who advised me that his anal glands needed emptying and it was neither serious, nor urgent, so would have to wait until they were open for that sort of appointment. I also informed her of Edna's death and the fact that Winston now belonged to me and should be registered at my address.

I then called her solicitor, Ms Hazel Menzies, to inform her of Edna's death and the fact I had her will and personal papers. As no meetings were taking place face-to-face, she read out Edna's will over the phone and I was truly touched to hear that she'd left me four thousand pounds, with the remaining funds to go to an animal charity she supported in North London. I believe that the Duchess of Sussex was their patron – or had been. I wasn't sure if they were still entitled to carry out their patronships. (They certainly shouldn't be, in my opinion.)

Other than clearing out Edna's place, the days passed without incident until Thursday, when there was another double coincidence – possibly in my favour. Some of the municipal tips had re-opened, and the body of the two-day-old baby girl was found in Needham Market. It was all over the news and the police were appealing for the mother to come forward for care, support and medical assistance. Maybe this investigation would take the pressure off mine. I'd heard nothing from the police since my visit to the station on Sunday, which was a relief, but there was an appeal for 'Assistance with a Police Investigation' in the Bury Free Press on Wednesday.

> "Last weekend a local man found a bag of rubbish on the roadside on the A143, six miles south of Bury-St-Edmunds. The bag was found to contain the bones of a premature baby, preserved in sawdust, estimated to be around forty years old. If anyone has any information that may assist our investigation, please contact Suffolk Police on 101, quoting CAD Ref. 549. Alternatively the charity Crimestoppers can be contacted anonymously, by calling 0800 444333, or on-line at https./crimestoppers-uk-org/give-information/forms. The Officer in charge of this case is Detective Chief Superintendent Richard Mayhew, who is based at the station in Raingate Street. Any information will be treated with the utmost confidentiality."

Oh my God, this put a new perspective on things. Why would someone want to dump the bones of a premature baby? There was obviously far more to this than I'd ever imagined, and now it seemed I was connected with a murder enquiry, but hopefully not the only suspect. Reading this prompted me to put a notice in the Bury Free Press to commemorate Edna. There was no need to give details of her funeral as I'd been told that only six mourners could be present, but I would be taking Winston, if it was allowed.

I didn't feel inclined to litter-pick in the circumstances, so I enlisted the help of Edna's other neighbour, Alan, to help me carry her furniture downstairs on Thursday afternoon. He was an okay sort of bloke and we were on reasonable terms.

"Did you read about that man who found a bag of bones on the A143?" Alan asked me as we were dismantling her bed. "I think I might be able to throw some light on that."

"Oh?" I asked, my heart skipping a beat. "How's that?"

"Was when my Nan lived in Wickhambrook, when I was a teenager. She lived in a largish detached house, but could often hear her neighbours having massive rows and there was some village gossip about their au pair having an affair with the man. Can't remember their names, but she was obviously pregnant. A pretty girl, she was – Swedish, I think, and much younger than him. I fancied the pants off her, but don't know what happened to the baby as it was never seen. Maybe she had it adopted. My Nan used to talk about it a lot as the marriage broke up and she stayed with the guy, but it's all rather a vague memory. May have been around 1982 or 1983, which could coincide with the dates. She moved to Haverhill around that time and is now dead, but my Mum may remember more about it. May have nothing whatsoever to do with this case, but just brought to mind that baby which was never seen."

As a problem-solver, I was instantly tempted to investigate it myself, but would need Alan's help. I had to do some quick thinking before giving my response. I was already far more involved in the case than I wished to be, but if I could solve the mystery it might vindicate me with the police. I made a hasty, but perhaps unwise decision.

"It was me who found that bag, Alan. You know how fanatical I am about litter, but please can you *not* mention to the fuzz that we've discussed this."

"Really, mate? Why not? Took your litter-picking a bit far, did you?"

"Because, with your help, I'd like to make my own

investigations, as the police are treating me like a suspect, and it could help clear my name."

"I hear what you're saying, but wouldn't that be considered meddling with a police matter?"

"I've done nothing wrong, Alan, and so my conscience is clear to do a bit of spade work, but only if it's entirely between ourselves at this stage. The appeal for information on the case was only published in the Bury Free yesterday. We've time on our hands."

"Alright, mate. I suppose there's no harm in following my hunch, but it's very vague."

"Thanks, Alan. Would you like to come round to mine for a beer when we've done this and we'll make a plan?"

* * *

I can't remember the last time anyone has been in my house, other than the police. Alan and I sat in my garden yesterday evening, downed several beers, and he told me about the fencing business he has with his brothers. Being as it's outdoors, he's still able to work. He rang me shortly after he returned home to say that he'd spoken to his mum and she remembered the people in Wickhambrook, so he drove me to Haverhill mid-morning to pay her a visit. I took a pen and notebook with me and felt like a proper detective on the case.

Jean lived on the ground floor of a small block of flats near the Sainsbury's superstore. She must have been in her late eighties, but her memory was sharp as a razor. We had a cup of socially-distanced tea in her garden and I complimented her on her window boxes.

"May I call you Billy?" she asked me.

"Of course. My dad was Bill, and I'm Billy."

"Alan says you're doing a bit of an investigation job, Billy."

"Well, I'm giving it a go, under the radar, with your and Alan's help, although I probably shouldn't be meddling in police business."

"I'll put my Miss Marple hat on then and tell you what I remember: it was 1982 and I know that for sure because it was the year I had my hysterectomy. After the operation, I went to stay in Wickhambrook with my mum to recuperate for a few weeks. Her neighbours, Phil and Diana Palmer, were always at it, rowing like, and their Swedish au pair was definitely pregnant. I think she was called Inga or Ingrid. It was while I was there that his wife left him, with their two young children. As you can imagine, it was quite a scandal in the small village in those days, and Inga/Ingrid was still there when my Mum died in 1998. The odd thing was though, that that baby was never seen. Talk was she'd had it adopted. The lady in the village post office may know a bit more, but I suppose you have to be careful who you talk to."

"And do you know if Mr Palmer still lives there?" I probed.

"I don't, I'm afraid. After Mum died her house was sold and I didn't visit Wickhambrook after that, but he lived at number nine Maple Gardens. Alan will remember. Are you going to pay him a visit on your way home?"

"I don't know, Jean. You've been very helpful, but it's all very tenuous and I'm already a bit out of my depth."

She asked me if I could take a look at a leaking tap in her bathroom. I told her it needed a new washer and that I'd be delighted to come over and fix it tomorrow, as I had no tools with me.

"What do you make of all that then, Billy?" Alan asked me on our way back. "Do you want to swing by Maple Gardens and have a butchers?"

"May as well. I do remember fitting a boiling water tap in Maple Gardens many years ago – maybe eleven or twelve. This is what Carl Jung called 'synchronicity'.

"What's that then?"

"It's a concept that Carl Jung introduced, which held that meaningful coincidences are a deeper connection with the universe – greater than our individual self – as if a message is conveyed by a higher power. It happens to me regularly."

"Wow. That's really weird."

Alan told me that he thought I was intelligent, which flattered me. No one had said that since I flunked by GCSE's, as I'd got in to dope in quite a big way as a teenager. It helped to ease my social deficiencies, but gave my parents a great deal of grief, and I think that's why they kept me at home. My mum was very over-protective and always treated me like a baby. I know from my studies of Carl Jung that an over-protective mother can cause a son problems in adult relationships, but to drive with Alan and chat, like having a friend, was a new thing to me and I was enjoying the experience. It seemed that my finding the bag has opened my life up.

I kept these thoughts to myself, but said to Alan, "I've always been interested in psychology – it was the only GCSE I got, apart from maths – and I know that my parents had aspirations that I would go into that profession. As it happens, I think I have done something with my life, but not intellectually. We could drive through Wickhambrook though, just to take a look."

As expected, number 9 Maple Gardens was the house where I had fitted the tap, so I told Alan.

"Now that really is weird, mate," he said. "My wife would be interested in that as she's into horoscopes, and that sort of thing. That poor bloke paid a high price for shagging his au pair, didn't he?"

There was a message on my home phone from the Undertakers saying that Edna's cremation had been booked for eleven a.m. next Tuesday at West Suffolk Crematorium, with only six mourners allowed to be present. This seemed like quick work to me, but when I called them back it was explained that bodies were no longer permitted to rest in the funeral parlours due to Covid 19, and that cremations were being arranged as quickly as possible to free up hospital mortuaries. I was also told that mourners must remain in their cars until the hearse arrived, and to keep two metres apart at all times. I was permitted to print out my own funeral sheets, which I would be responsible for distributing. But the good news was that I was allowed to take Winston, if he was kept on a lead and well behaved. They were not able to provide a floral tribute either, due to the florists being closed.

Although not the cheapest option, I chose a wicker coffin because I think Edna would have liked that. She had thoughtfully pre-paid all her funeral costs. Of course, the hearse was obligatory, but I didn't want any funeral cars, which was just as well as they, too, were out of commission. She also said that under the circumstances the deceased wouldn't be able to be dressed in their own special clothes, but I would be allowed to bring something of Edna's to drape over her coffin if I did it myself at the crematorium. I then rang Social Services and asked them to let Edna's carers know about the arrangements, but only a maximum of three could attend, as I was sure that Alan and his wife would want to be there.

I felt drained after that and had a nip of Scotch to perk me up. I heated up some sausage rolls and oven chips, then Winston and I spent the afternoon watching Fawlty Towers. I think it was the best sit-com ever written and it always lifts my spirits to watch Basil, Sybil, Manuel and Polly clowning about. Classic comedy.

I drove to Haverhill on Saturday morning to fix Jean's tap, and came back via Wickhambrook as I'd had rather a brainwave about my reason for visiting Mr Palmer. I started thinking about Barry Manilow as I left Jean's and, sure enough, 'Mandy' came on the radio just as I was approaching the village. I'd always liked Barry Manilow, and had all his cassettes. I stopped my car just short of my destination to listen to the end of the song.

Maple Terrace was a small, sixties brick development near the church. I never forget where I've done a job. Number nine had a For Sale board outside, with a Sold sticker over it. A man, probably in his early seventies, was cleaning a vintage Triumph Herald on his forecourt.

"Mr Palmer?" I called out, winding down the window.

The man squeezed out his chamois leather and approached my van.

"Can I help you?" he asked.

"Billy Pooley. I'm sure you won't remember me, but I fitted a hot water tap for you many years ago, and there have been several problems with the design of the model you've got. With time on my hands, I thought I'd do a bit of research on the units I fitted to see whether they've caused my customers any difficulties."

As he drew nearer, I could see his left hand, which was shaking, had obviously been severely burnt.

"See this?" he said. "That's what that tap did to me, but it was probably my fault as I never really learnt how to use it properly.

I never used it again. We only got it at the insistence of my then partner, who was Swedish. You know what Scandinavians are like about hygiene and modern gadgets." He seemed to be very nice about it.

"Design and mechanism have come a long way since then, Sir, and the modern taps have many more features and are much safer and easier to use now," I reassured him.

"I hope you haven't called to get more business out of me, Mr Pooley, because my house sold just before the lockdown and I'm moving out in a couple of weeks to be nearer my grandchildren in Nottingham."

I couldn't possibly ask him about his grandchildren, and hadn't a clue how I was going to conclude the conversation, which Mr Palmer kindly did for me.

"It's kind and conscientious of you to take the trouble to call in, Mr Pooley. I appreciate it. Good day now."

I could have killed for a cold beer in a nice pub garden, but instead went back home to make my next move, which was to inform Crimestoppers anonymously.

Thankfully, it occurred to me just before I dialled the number that I couldn't do it myself for fear of voice recognition as all calls were surely recorded. I didn't think I had any more to contribute to my investigation, but felt that what I did know was worth reporting. I wrote down what I wished to say and took it round to Alan's, as I was sure he wouldn't mind doing it for me. Short, but to the point:

This message is for the attention of Chief Superintendent Richard Mayhew, Suffolk Police, CAD reference number 549. I have a possible lead on this case, which is the unexplained absence/disappearance of a baby born around March 1982 to a Swedish au-pair, Inga or Ingrid, who had become pregnant by her employer, a Mr Philip Palmer of 9 Maple Terrace, Wickhambrook.

Alan was out on a job when I called, but his wife invited me in for a cup of coffee and offered to make the call. I reminded her to dial 1571 first. She said it was the most exciting thing that had happened to her for ages, to be part of a murder mystery. I told her that I'd fixed Jean's tap and paid a visit to Mr Palmer under the guise of concern over a water softener I'd fitted many years previously.

"Oh, how clever, Billy. You should've been a detective yourself. Alan says you have lots of coincidences and I think that's really interesting. Of course, I can't do my hairdressing business at the moment, but I hear loads of stories like that from my clients. They definitely happen to some people, but not others."

I said I would lend her one of my Carl Jung books, and also gave her the details of Edna's cremation. When I got home, I rang the hospital and was happy to hear that Dad was out of Intensive Care and on a private, barriered ward, and was making a good recovery from Covid 19. I felt guilty for not giving him more thought.

* * *

On Sunday, I went to Tesco to buy several packets of sandwiches and multi-packs of crisps and snacks, Prosecco, wine and beer for Edna's wake. That way, people could open their own sandwiches and crisps and it would be totally hygienic and safe. I also bought paper napkins, plastic tumblers and wine goblets, all of which were disposable. I'd taken my suit and tie to be dry cleaned, and when Tuesday arrived, I was looking pretty smart. I dressed Winston in the red bow tie I used to wear as a young child and took along one of Edna's many crocheted blankets to lay over her coffin, along with a bunch of mixed, colourful flowers bought at a petrol station.

The cremation was attended by Alan, Julie, and three of her carers. I knew two of them. Edna came in to some suitable recorded soft music, and the Celebrant welcomed us and read out the Lord's Prayer. Before listening to 'Somewhere Over the Rainbow'. I gave a short tribute of what I knew about Edna's life, and my memories of her and her daughter, Denise, who used to babysit me. As Edna's coffin glided through the curtains we listened to 'We'll Meet Again', sung by Vera Lynn, who was one of her heroines. I think that Edna would have been pleased with the service, although it was a quick and rather impersonal affair and was all over in twenty minutes, but everyone came back to mine afterwards. Fortunately, as the weather was still warm we were able to be in the garden. Everyone thought my safe, individually-packed catering was ingenious and I impressed them with an unusual piece of knowledge that every single packet of crisps has an expiry date on a Saturday. The sun, combined with Prosecco, wine and beer had the effect of making everyone quite merry and I think it was a good 'do', although it was rather odd that the first time I'd ever entertained in my life would be a wake.

They all left around three o'clock, but the night carer, called Mandy stayed on, and we downed several more drinks. I didn't know her but felt a connection. She was very large, with a pretty face, a dimple on her chin and sort of magenta-coloured long hair, tied in a high pony tail with a butterfly clip. She also had a lot of piercings and was wearing a long, flowing tie-died purple dress. For the first time since I was a teenager, I felt a crashing desire for sex and, fuelled by booze, we ended up on my settee, trying to kiss and so on. It was all rather a fumble. I would never have had the courage without a fair bit of alcohol inside me. She said if she'd known she'd get lucky she would have worn nicer underwear, and not 'married pants'. I didn't really notice though, nor did I know what 'married pants' were. I didn't ask her if she was married, but she wasn't wearing a wedding or engagement ring. She had a huge knuckle-duster of a skull and crossbones ring on her left index finger, which I found rather sinister. I remember asking her if she liked Barry Manilow and she said he was rather old-fashioned, but we laughed. I couldn't get my head around to tell her about the coincidence of hearing 'Mandy' on the radio recently.

An ice cream van was tinkling in the street, so I went to get us some '99's and she made us a mug of tea and cleared away the stuff from the garden. She's a homely sort of girl, rather like my mother, and must be a good ten years younger than me.

Then there was the question of her getting home, since neither of us was in a fit state to drive. She lived out of town, but didn't want to get a taxi because of being a key-worker and the certainty of germs, so things stood to be in my favour. Once again, Edna had opened up my life in a most unexpected way. Winston was sleeping in his bed and still had his dicky bow on, so I got him up and we all went for a walk to the Abbey Gardens.

There wasn't much litter, but I did pick up a video of 'Four Weddings and a Funeral' from the top of a bin. I told her about my litter-picking and I think it impressed her. She told me that she wasn't married and lived with a co-worker in a cottage in Fornham All Saints, a few miles north of Bury. Her hobbies were dress-making, needlework, cats and chinchillas. She also said that she'd tried internet dating, but it wasn't that successful.

I'm not fond of cats (and don't know anything about chinchillas) and as my small talk isn't incredibly cultivated, we walked quite a way in silence. I was a little unsure of how the rest of the day would pan out, but she suggested getting fish and chips later on, which seemed promising. I left her to choose a DVD to watch while I went upstairs to change in to some shorts and have a quick wash, although I think I overdid the after-shave a bit to disguise my sweating.

When I came downstairs there was a message on my answerphone.

"Good afternoon, Mr. Pooley. Superintendent Richard Mayhew speaking. We've recently received a lead through Crimestoppers and today interviewed a man from Wickhambrook, who has confessed to depositing the black bag you found. Might you be able to call me back to arrange coming in to the station tomorrow? Thank you."

"I couldn't help overhearing your message, Billy. What was that all about?" Mandy asked as I came downstairs. I'd really have preferred *not* explaining it at that moment.

"Rather a long story, but a relief that the police may have solved the mystery of a bag of rubbish I found and picked up from the edge of the A143 nearly two weeks ago. It was a stupid thing to do – and particularly because it contained the very old bones of a premature baby."

"Oh, how awful. Were you under suspicion then?"

"Not really, but the police didn't treat me very well."

"Poor Billy, how distressing. You're such a kind and gentle man to be involved with anything like that. I'll go and pour us a drink while you ring the station. Beer or wine?"

We sat in the garden, but the timing of that call had really put a dampener on the proceedings, even though I should have been relieved. It certainly sobered me up though, and I was ready for that beer. Mandy brought her chair closer to mine.

"I hope you're not feeling bad about today, Billy, in case we acted hastily? I don't feel bad about it as we'd both had rather a lot to drink."

I was touched by her honesty and sensitivity. "Of course not, but it's all been quite a day, what with Edna's funeral, having people here, and I feel a bit out of my comfort zone. That's all. Sorry, but I'm really quite a loner."

"I can see that, and that's why I like you. You're a genuine guy, and that's a rarity. Try and forget about the bag and we'll walk to the chippy together. I'm hungry."

* * *

Last night was uneventful as the frisson had left me, and the shed load of booze I'd consumed may have affected my performance, which I was of course nervous about anyway, as a virgin. I wasn't confident to take things further, but Mandy was understanding and agreed that we shouldn't rush things. I lent her a T-shirt and she slept in my spare room. I went to bed feeling that I'd failed both of us and possibly blown my chances.

After showering the following morning, I took Mandy a mug of tea, and was aware of my tatty dressing gown and worn, smelly slippers. We sat together for a while on her bed and she took my hand.

"Don't feel badly about yesterday, Billy. All this is rather new to me too, but I really do want to see you again. I have to work tonight, so won't stay long as I generally rest in the afternoons before a night shift. You did such a good job with Edna's funeral and wake, and when this police business is out of the way you'll feel much less stressed."

I couldn't believe her generosity and how my life seemed to have turned around in less than twenty-four hours. While she took a shower, I cooked us eggs and bacon, and she left shortly after we'd exchanged mobile numbers. An arrangement was made to meet up on Friday at her cottage.

I got to the police station at eleven and met Mayhew, who was a great deal more cordial, and our conversation wasn't recorded. He explained that an anonymous call to Crimestoppers had given them a lead to visit a man, who lived in Wickhambrook. The man had revealed that his girlfriend, a former au-pair, had given birth prematurely to a stillborn baby in their house in 1982. For various reasons, the girlfriend hadn't seen a doctor about her pregnancy, but he thought the baby was probably born around thirty weeks. Mayhew informed me that the man didn't need to register the birth of a premature baby at the time. Since then the law has changed and you must register the birth of a stillborn baby at twenty-four weeks or over. The story had been verified by the man's ex-girlfriend, who's now living in London, and DNA wasn't going to be pursued.

I asked why the man had dumped the bag, and Mayhew said that he was about to move house and didn't want to take it with him. He'd planned to take the bag to the tip, under normal circumstances. They'd considered burying the baby in their back garden, but didn't want a fox to dig it up. Instead they laid their baby to rest in pine sawdust in a small cardboard box; pine sawdust having preservative qualities and it would take care of odours from the decomposing body.

"Do you know what, Mr Pooley?" Mayhew said. "There are sometimes grey areas in our dealings and we like to show compassion if we can. If you lose a baby now after twenty-four weeks, the body must be cremated by law. Also fly-tipping carries a penalty – up to fifty thousand pounds for dumping white goods, or a year's imprisonment if convicted by a Magistrates' Court. Four hundred pounds is now the fixed penalty notice for small-scale fly-tipping, which I'm going to waive. That man has Parkinson's, and has also lived with this guilty secret for thirty-eight years, without any counselling or support for him or his girlfriend. Those were different times. But it seems his story all ties up and we've now closed the case. I'd like to thank you for your co-operation and your time."

I walked out of that station feeling that a huge burden had been lifted and wished it was this time yesterday. As I drove home, my thoughts turned to Mandy. And I thought about her for most of the rest of the day, making my stomach sort of turn over. This was something new to me, and maybe that's what 'being in love' is. I got straight on the net when I got back and ordered myself a dressing gown, slippers, a couple of pairs of pyjamas, a pair of Chino's, some long shorts and two short-sleeved shirts from Next. The weather had turned, so I ate the remaining sandwiches in front of the telly and put on the video of 'Four Weddings and a Funeral'. I still had a video player, but the advertised sleeve didn't contain the film, but was a home-made porn video of oriental lesbians having sex. Of course, I watched it, and found it quite arousing.

A nurse from West Suffolk Hospital rang me later on to say that my Dad was now recovered and would be clapped out by all the staff mid-morning on Friday and taken by ambulance back to his care home. I would be welcome to see him outside the hospital doors at a safe distance, and that it might be filmed and featured on BBC LookEast, after the evening news. This was not the outcome I'd expected either. Edna, Carl Jung, or my higher power – someone – was definitely looking after me. I felt blessed.

I couldn't resist ringing Mandy to tell her both bits of good news, and she agreed to come with me to clap Dad out on Friday. I can't remember feeling happier in my life, so it seemed a good moment to have a few beers to celebrate.

As I was feeling lonely, but confident, I impulsively knocked on Alan's door to tell him about my eventful day and to lend Marie my Carl Jung book. They invited me in for a drink.

"You're a dark horse, aren't you?" Alan said. "Did we not see one of the carers leaving your house this morning? Did you score?"

This confused me. "We had a fun time, and I may have got myself a girlfriend."

"Good man. We thought you were gay! You gave Edna a great send-off on Tuesday, too. Seems that things are looking up for you, and that your synchronicity's working."

* * *

I couldn't wait until Friday to see Mandy again. We'd arranged that I would be at her cottage quite early, before going to see Dad heralded out by the staff of West Suffolk hospital mid-morning. I'd taken along a picnic lunch of beers, samosas, pitta bread, dips and strawberries, and one of Edna's many crocheted rugs to sit on.

Mandy introduced me to her four black and white cats: Eenie, Meenie and Minie, and Dave – the old boy. She told me that a friend of hers had found the four abandoned young kittens last year in a cardboard box next to a bottle bank in Bury. She'd raised the kittens by hand, but Mo, the runt, didn't make it.

"Dave's getting on and gets a bit crabby with the youngsters. He came to us as a stray, and never left. This is Cilla, my chinchilla. She's recently been mated by Monty, but I don't know if she's taken. Their gestation period is fifteen weeks, which is a long time for a small animal. He's only a year old, and this was a virgin-mate, so fingers crossed. Here he is. They have to be kept separate."

My sympathies were with Monty. I made the right noises to admire her animal collection, but the chinchillas' cages did smell a bit!

"What do they eat?" I asked, needing to show positive interest.

"Pretty much everything – berries, twigs, fruit, herbs, meat and oats. They have to be kept at a heat of just under seventy degrees at all times, so I've invested massively in this Dyson fan to keep them cool – or warm, if necessary." I admired the state-of-the art fan, and then we had a cup of coffee in her garden before setting off for the hospital.

Although I'd been advised of the approximate time, we had to hang around for ages outside the main exit of the hospital before Dad appeared. We couldn't see what was going on inside, but out he came, with his nurses, to a huge round of applause. The LookEast film crew were there and they interviewed me. I felt emotional, and so proud of him. We weren't allowed to touch, but I introduced him to Mandy, and he was smiling, waving and dribbling.

Mandy and I found a cornfield not too far out of town and I had my first romantic picnic. I think she enjoyed it too. It being hot and me being nervous, I got a bit light-headed and told her about the sexy video I'd picked up as I was feeling her pendulous breasts. She laughed and said that it would be fun to watch the video together, as she'd been involved in those sort of dealings, so we went back to mine. Naturally, my imagination wasn't the only thing to be aroused. I was intrigued, as any man would be.

* * *

Covid and 2020 changed my life forever. A poor little foetus lost before its time and I think of Inga/Ingrid – now that Mandy might be carrying ours.

DESIRE 2019

I am one hundred percent heterosexual and had a handsome partner to prove it. Also a previous husband, although not quite so handsome. He decided to change horses and become gay, so we parted after eight years of marriage. I'd no idea. It was all rather humiliating, but we did produce two beautiful daughters: Imogen and Kate. Kate is now twenty and reading English at Oxford, having inherited her father's literary talents. When she was fifteen, in 2014, we made a trip to Amsterdam for the weekend in the Easter holidays to research her history GCSE project on the life of Anne Frank. That was the beginning of my love affair with Holland.

PART 1

I booked us into a small, boutique hotel, The Galilei on Singel, near the flower market. This was my choice as I'd qualified at Paula Pryke's Floristry School in the nineties and wanted to be near the market, which was a daily injection of colourful joy to me. We visited Anne Frank's house/museum twice during our three-day stay. It was both enlightening and depressing, a strange combination, but Kate got an A* for her efforts. On our second visit, she wanted to stay on to study the photographs and choose some books for her research, so I went back to the hotel via a coffee shop (not the hash-smoking sort). I was slightly apprehensive that Kate would want to visit one, as she could easily have passed for eighteen, but she was studious and not as adventurous as Imogen, who was doing her A levels that June and hoping to read psychology at Aberdeen, where her father, Russell, lives.

Back at the hotel, I was engrossed with the fish tank in the foyer. A small, yellow fish endlessly made the same journey around the tank: starting with swimming under the little bridge and then right to circle the tank, before repeating the process over and over. I'd seen a tiger doing that at London Zoo and it is, I believe, stress-related behaviour. My preoccupation was interrupted by a good-looking Dutch man, wearing a Mandarin-collared pale blue shirt, stone-coloured chinos and suede loafers. He introduced himself as Marius van den Berg, owner of the hotel. He had flawless English, as the Dutch so often do.

"Do you like our fish tank?" he asked me.

"Yes, but I think the little yellow one is stressed because of his repetitive behaviour. See the way he constantly makes the same journey around the tank?"

"You're very observant; I hadn't noticed that before. Are you enjoying your stay here, and I hope you've everything you need?"

"I'm loving it, thank you," I replied. "How do you do? Leonora Johnston – Leo. And such a clever touch to leave the little bottles of perfume on our pillows on our first night. They say that you never forget the association of smell with place and time. A clever bit of marketing!"

Marius offered me a coffee or a glass of the house champagne. I don't normally drink at lunchtime, but accepted a glass of champagne, as I was on holiday. We chatted about the hotel and how long he'd owned it. He was easy to talk to, and I asked him who did his beautiful flower arrangements in the reception, foyer and bedrooms.

"My cousin's responsible for the flowers, but she's just started having chemo-therapy for her cancer, so I'm not sure how much longer she can carry on working."

"I'm a professional florist in London," I told him, feeling a bit heady and confident after the second glass of champagne.

"How interesting. Might you consider moving your talents to Amsterdam?" he flirted.

I laughed. "This is my first visit to Holland, so I don't know about that."

Marius asked me if I'd been to the Rijksmuseum as it currently had a controversial Rembrandt/Auerbach exhibition, only running until the fourteenth of April. "It's best to book your tickets at reception, so you won't have to queue. Where else are you planning to visit before you go?" he asked.

"My daughter's researching Anne Frank for her GSCE project, but apart from that we don't have any plans. I love the flower market, of course, and we do want to eat Indonesian food. Tonight's our last evening."

"May I suggest the Indrapura restaurant on Rembrandtplein – only a twelve-minute walk away. It's a wonderful experience and I'd be very happy to take you and your daughter there for dinner. It would be my pleasure."

The Dutch are so friendly and welcoming, I thought. That sort of invitation would never be issued in London. So I agreed and we met in reception at seven. They eat early in Holland.

The Indrapura put on an incredible culinary feast: all the variety of many exotic, fragrant and spicy dishes – nothing like we'd ever tasted.

"My real passion is sailing," Marius told us over dinner. "I keep a small yacht at Veere in Zeeland, one of the islands south of Rotterdam, and I have a holiday home in Haamstede in the shadow of the lighthouse. It's a very romantic place, with wonderful sandy dunes and beaches, about two hours away by car. I go there most weekends during the summer months, and for Christmas. It's the most beautiful and special place in the world – better even than the Caribbean."

"That sounds amazing," I said. "I'd love to return to Holland."

"So, is this a girls' trip? No Papa?" Marius asked while we were eating our mango and pineapple sorbets.

"It's always a girls' trip in our family – just me, Kate and Imogen. Imogen is two years older than Kate and they both go to Channing, a school in Highgate, near where we live. Their father decided to take a different path in life and now lives in Scotland with his partner, Martin, a clothes designer."

"I see."

We didn't go any further with that topic in view of Kate's presence, but the girls do have a good relationship with their father, a credit both to them and him.

I felt an attraction to Marius and wondered if he felt the same. It seemed he did.

When we got back to the hotel, I ordered breakfast in our room as it was our last day and we needed to pack. Our tray duly arrived with an envelope containing a hand-written note from Marius:

'I so enjoyed your company last night and it would be my pleasure to take you to the Rijksmuseum at eleven o'clock, if that suits you. Please let Reception know if you would like to come.'

Marius.

Kate wasn't keen to traipse around looking at Dutch masters, and wanted one last visit to Anne Frank's house, so we agreed to meet back at the hotel at two before leaving for the airport.

"Looks like you've got yourself a date, Mum. Well done!"

It was good to have Kate's approval as I haven't exactly been inundated with romance since Russell and I parted. Imogen would have been a different matter – she can be quite critical and headstrong, like her father.

As we travelled to the museum by tram, I asked Marius if he was always so attentive to his guests.

"Absolutely not, Leo, but I was intrigued by your interest in the fish tank, and you're a very attractive woman." For the first time in years I felt myself blushing, but I didn't enquire about his marital circumstances.

The exhibition, only running for ten more days, was 'Rembrandt-Auerbach: Raw Truth'. The collection included their own Rembrandts, plus six imported ones. I'd never heard of Frank Auerbach before, and don't know much about art. The careful, sensitive and sincere studies by Rembrandt contrasted massively with Auerbach's bold, pungent and paint-laden ones. It was hard to find the subject amongst the chaos of massed ribbons and ripples of layered paint. There were three hundred and twenty-five years between their birth dates, and I felt ignorant for not seeing the connection. We learnt that Auerbach was born to German-Jewish parents in 1931, and sent to England when he was eight years old in 1939 to escape the Nazis. He never saw his parents again; they died in concentration camps. This information helped to explain his disturbing paintings, and he was still alive, aged eighty three. Marius told me that Auerbach had become friends with Lucien Freud, some ten years his senior, and had clearly been influenced by him. The Rijksmuseum is huge, and, after a coffee in the on-site café, we wandered around a few more galleries before I reached saturation point. The Dutch have much to be proud of with their art history, but to me they are all much the same – like the frescoes in Florence.

Marius was insistent that we have a local delicacy for lunch, but it would be nothing fancy. We walked to a nearby square to a food stall selling herring *broodjes*, little white buns. We ate on plastic chairs by the kiosk and the salty juice from the brioche bun, crammed with fish and pickles, burst as I took my first mouthful, splashing my shirt and down my chin. I didn't know whether to be embarrassed or amused. Being English, I opted for embarrassment. Marius gallantly dabbed my face with a non-absorbent paper napkin.

"I hope you've enjoyed your stay, Leo, and that you'll want to come back to Amsterdam?" Marius asked me as we walked back to the hotel. "Maybe when the weather gets warmer, I could show you my holiday home and yacht."

"That sounds very tempting, Marius, but I have to get the girls through their exams, so maybe not until late June."

"That's a long time away," he replied.

Kate was waiting for us by the fish tank and was very excited.

"Mummy, they were having a workshop for students today on 'Heroism vs. Anti-Semitism'. There's another one in a fortnight, over a weekend, and it's in English. Please, please, please Mummy, can I go to it? I met a girl called Anneliese, who is also doing a project on Anne Frank and we're going to compare notes. It'll give me a real insight from the Dutch point of view. We've exchanged email addresses."

"We'll have to think about that, sweetheart, and see what we can do."

After a final departing coffee in the Lounge, Marius instructed a porter to get our luggage. He produced a beautifully wrapped box, which I had to take as hand luggage as it was too big to fit in my suitcase.

"This is to be a memory of your time in Amsterdam, and I've ordered you a taxi to Schiphol, which is waiting outside. All paid for, and I look forward to welcoming you both back. Do let me know your dates." We exchanged three kisses (the Dutch way) and Marius called out, "*Tot ziens*," as he shut our taxi door.

Unbeknown to Kate she was playing Cupid, and had given me a reason to return. I tried to absorb the rapid events of the past twenty-four hours on the aeroplane, while Kate was reading her new books. Just as life is chugging along, unexpected happenings conspire to change things. I recalled the proverb by Charles Swindoll: 'Life is ten per cent what happens to you, and ninety per cent how you respond to it.' Russell was fond of proverbs.

Marius hadn't asked me for my contact details, but he could easily get that information from my booking, and I think he knew we'd be back.

In fact we returned two weeks later. Fortunately, I had flowers to do for a friend's daughter's wedding at the church of St. Bartholomew the Great in the Barbican over the first weekend, which gave me a distraction and a focus. It was a lovely time of year for yellow and white spring flowers, and Imogen and Kate helped me assemble the bridesmaids' and flower girls' posies, while I did the bride's bouquet, the church decorations, and also arrangements for the reception at The Merchant Taylors Company.

Marius's gift contained an indoor planting kit of mixed tulip bulbs in a tasteful hemp planter, as it was too late in the season to be planting outside. The week before we left, and after a slightly boozy lunch at Carluccio's in St Christopher's Place with my friend Colette, I uncharacteristically and impulsively splashed out nearly three hundred quid on a denim pinafore dress, jeans, and a shirt from Whistles. Also some pale blue suede ankle boots, surely destined to attract disaster. Not that Marius would know any of my clothes, but it always feels good to spend and spoil yourself when you're in a high and expectant mood. Kate had been e-mailing Anneliese, exchanging essays and ideas, and Anneliese had invited her to stay on the Saturday evening. I must admit to having some nagging doubts, as the path ahead seemed too good to be true, so I tried not to raise my hopes.

I booked our flights for the following Friday evening, and also the Galilei for two nights, with instructions to inform Marius of our arrival. Due to a security issue of an unattended rucksack near one of the check-ins prior to our arrival at Stansted, our flight was delayed by nearly two hours, so we didn't arrive at the hotel until midnight. Marius had arranged to leave an assortment of cold meats, cheeses, fruit and bread in our room. And a bottle of rosé, which was very thoughtful.

I'd no idea what the agenda would be for the weekend, but I walked Kate to Anne Frank's house for registration and to meet Anneliese and her mother at nine thirty on Saturday morning. It was a beautiful and cloudless day, warm for the time of year, so I wore my new jeans and shirt. As it was still early, I went to the same coffee shop to pass the time. My mother always said that it was wise to keep a keen man waiting. Marius was at reception when I got back to the hotel, and his eyes lit up when he saw me.

"Welcome back, Leo. How lovely to see you. I'm sorry to hear you had a late arrival yesterday, but if you're not too tired I have a surprise day out for us. My car's outside, when you're ready."

"That sounds lovely, Marius." I felt like a gauche teenager as I touched up my make-up in the downstairs loo. His open-topped Mercedes drove us through the industrial areas of Amsterdam, giving way to verdant, irrigated countryside, with flat fields, dykes and windmills. After about an hour, we reached the incredible Keukenhof Gardens in Lisse, with its four pavilions and masses of tulips, hyacinths, daffodils, carnations, irises and lilies, all in wonderfully planted paths and formations. Marius told me it was the world's largest spring garden – some seven million flowers. I thought it was exquisite. We then drove through the colour-coded tulip fields – a massive mosaic of magnificent blooms, all in their prime. It was as if I had been seeing life in monochrome until I saw those fields; it blew my mind.

"I thought you'd enjoy this," Marius said. "They're at their very best now and will be harvested any day. Your timing's perfect."

I thanked him for my bulbs, and he told me that tulips were originally cultivated in the Ottoman Empire and imported to Holland in the sixteenth century.

"When Carolus Clusius, a pioneering botanist in that time,

wrote the first major book on tulips in 1592, they became so popular that his garden was regularly raided and bulbs stolen. Also, during the Second World War, the impoverished and starving Dutch ate tulip bulbs to keep them alive."

"How dreadful." It was all so interesting; I had no idea that tulips didn't originate from Holland.

"You must be hungry, Leo. I'm going to introduce you to one of our favourite national dishes: croquettes. I don't think you can get them in England." We stopped at a timbered hostelry overlooking the tulip fields, where we sat at an outside table with green umbrellas, advertising Heineken beer. Marius ordered a selection of prawn, meat and cheese croquettes and a salad, to be washed down with half a pint of Heineken and a bowl of frites.

"Very Dutch," he said. "Do you like them?"

"I'm not sure," I replied honestly. They all tasted much the same, and were rather like giant, potatoe-y rolled fish fingers. A moment on the lips, a lifetime on the hips.

"Do you have plans this evening?" he enquired.

I deliberately hadn't mentioned that Kate was staying with Anneliese, waiting to see how the day panned out, and I couldn't decide whether to tell him or not. I decided against it.

"There's an excellent Thai restaurant we could go to, if you like Thai food?"

"That sounds lovely. Thank you, Marius."

After lunch we walked through the water meadows, where Frisian cattle paddled and drank from the narrow dykes. Marius took my hand.

"There's a very famous Dutch children's book: *The Cow who fell in the Canal*," he told me. Every Dutch child reads it. Hendrika, the cow, falls into the canal by her field and travels to market in a floating raft to see the sights. You would love the local markets, with all the cheeses and flower stalls."

On the way back to the hotel I suddenly felt tired and needed a rest and a lengthy soak in the bath. Marius quite understood.

"I'll meet you in reception at seven then, Leo, if that's alright. Have a good rest now."

I rang Imogen, who was spending the weekend with a friend, and told her about my day.

"You be careful, Mum, without Kate as your chaperone tonight, and don't do anything I wouldn't do!"

More often than not, it seemed that our roles were reversed – with Imogen my mother, and me her daughter. She's a much stronger character than I am.

Marius had gone to a lot of trouble to arrange things, which I appreciated, but I started to feel that I was losing control of the situation. He had impeccable manners and was very good-looking, but almost too perfect and considerate. His brown hair with a hint of grey, was side-parted, and he was tall, slim and clean-shaven. He reminded me of a character out of *The Great Gatsby*. The more I thought about it, I couldn't be sure whether I fancied him or not, which disappointed me. But I was tired and needed rest and time alone. I slept for far too long, so only had time for a quick shower before we met.

"Where's Kate?" he asked me at reception. I then had to explain that she was staying with her new Dutch friend, Anneliese, for the night.

"Would you like to walk through the red-light district? It's on the way to the restaurant."

"Not particularly, unless you can recommend it!" I joked, testing his sense of humour.

"It's just that most people who visit Amsterdam are curious, that's all."

"Alright then."

The red-light district wasn't a very pleasant experience – narrow alleyways of small, brightly-lit cubicles, with overweight, naked housewives showing off their wares, legs akimbo. Some of them had black S.M. leather gear on, and all wore bright red lipstick. The cubicles with curtains drawn were obviously occupied.

"What about AIDS?" I asked Marius.

"I presume they all insist on contraception," he replied.

It was all rather sordid and not in the least bit arousing, if that was his intention. Minutes later, we were greeted at the restaurant with bows and genuflections, and I was presented with a purple orchid headpiece to clip in my hair, with a matching buttonhole given to Marius. The restaurant, already busy, was dimly-lit, with plush red velvet banquettes, heavy, dark furniture and an elaborately carved wooden screen along one wall.

"Good evening, Meneer Marius. Your usual table is ready. Good evening, lady. Please, come this way."

"Thank you, Kannika."

"You seem to be very well known here, Marius," I observed, a little jealously.

"Two of Kannika's sisters do cleaning at the hotel. They're such hard workers and so honest. I like to patronise the restaurant, but am usually on my own."

At that moment, a bowl of prawn crackers, surrounded by elaborately carved carrots and radishes arrived at our table, with two bowls of sauces.

"This one hot, lady," said Kannika, pointing to one of the

bowls of chilli, making a small bow, with her hands in a praying position. "Be careful, and enjoy."

Marius ordered us prawn and chicken Tom-Yum soups, followed by fried squid with a green papaya salad, chicken satay, pad Thai noodles and stir-fried bok choy with garlic, ginger and lime.

"You certainly know how to spoil a girl, Marius. This is all truly delicious."

"I don't think you enjoyed the croquettes at lunch, so I hope this makes up for it."

"You said you generally come here on your own?" I probed.

"Yes. You've been very British and polite and not asked me about my circumstances, so I will tell you. That is if you want to know." I nodded, not wanting to sound too anxious.

"I thought I had a good marriage with my wife, Cornelia, but I was working very hard in the hotel business at that time, and trying to make enough money to open one of my own. I spent all my weekends and time off sailing, and she didn't enjoy being on the water. It was my parents who owned the house in Schouwen-Duiveland, by the lighthouse, and we often had friends to stay so that Cornie wouldn't be lonely. She also started drinking heavily. It was probably all my fault. The divorce deal was that I kept the Kleine Vuurtoren, the country house, and my boat, Mathilde. Cornelia kept our town house opposite The Galilei, and a big chunk of my money. She took up with some guy she met in AA. We've been divorced about four years now, and our son, Kees, is in his final year at Breda University, studying Hotel Management. That's it really. I've since bought myself a flat not far from the hotel, and have busied myself with work to get over it. We're on reasonable terms now, as we have to be for Kees. Fortunately, Cornie and Fons, her boyfriend, have moved out of Amsterdam, so I don't see them so much. I was very heartbroken and made a promise to myself that I will never lose a beautiful woman again, and will be more attentive. That's enough, but now you know my situation. I'm sorry if I bored you."

"Not at all, Marius. You're a very kind and sensitive man. It all sounds horrid."

The soups arrived, and our conversation and attention were then diverted to the food.

Walking back to the hotel, he asked me if I'd like to have a drink at his flat, which I accepted. He put on a compendium of classical music, starting with Ravel's Bolero, and opened a bottle of Champagne.

His flat was spacious, but minimally furnished, with comfortable grey sofas, oak flooring, Persian rugs and modern art. Two large colourful prints of Chairman Mao were signed by Andy Warhol, and I asked him if they were original.

"Yes, I inherited them from my uncle, who was unmarried, and a friend of his. He also lived in New York. I think they may have had a relationship, but it was never discussed. I've got some of his Campbell Soup ones in the kitchen."

"They must be very valuable. This music reminds me of Torvill and Dean, and their beautiful skating harmony." I was starting to feel very relaxed.

"Yes. When the canals in Amsterdam freeze, the skating's so much fun. Every Dutch person can skate. They last froze in 2012, but it happens less frequently now, due to global warming."

Marius had just settled himself on the sofa and put his arm around me when my mobile rang. It was Lucas, Anneliese's father.

"I'm sorry to interrupt your evening, Leonora, but Kate's had a fall on the pavement and I'm afraid she's concussed. She has since vomited and I'm not too worried. I'm an anaesthetist and I don't think there is any need for her to go to hospital, but I think you should come and collect her now. I'm so sorry."

That made the decision for the night, which was a slight relief as I had no clean clothes or toiletries with me. Marius drove me to their house and then drove Kate and me back to the hotel. She was still a bit groggy, but seemed fine in the morning.

As much as I'd enjoyed Marius's company, I needed a bit of space and wanted to explore the shops on Sunday morning, so I texted him after dropping Kate off for the last day of her seminar. He replied immediately and suggested we have a simple lunch and then go on a city-tour boat trip. I shopped at Zara and bought dungarees for the girls, and went to a delightfully old-fashioned stationery shop to have some personalised cards made up while I had a coffee. We lunched at a small café and ate *poffertjes* – delicious small thin Dutch pancakes with lemon, sugar and cream, before making our way back to the boat's boarding station next to the hotel. Marius had booked one of the more luxurious cruisers, with comfortable seating and a bar. Whilst waiting for our boat, one docked advertising in big block letters a romantic cruise through the canals. Only a fender was covering the 'C' of canal, thereby screaming 'LOVERS ANAL CRUISES'. We laughed.

By the time Kate got back to the hotel, I'd packed, and we were ready to go. There was no bill, so I suggested to Marius when he was driving us to Schiphol that he should come and stay with us in Highgate for some reciprocal hospitality.

Kate admitted on the flight back that Anneliese's brother had taken them to a dope café and they'd shared a joint. This must have accounted for her fall, which I was very angry about, but was surely my own fault for not checking with her mother what they'd be doing after the seminar finished. I'd been more pre-occupied with my own pleasure. Out of guilt, I decided not to take it up with them.

Marius came over three weeks later. I put him in the spare room, as our first intimate encounter couldn't possibly take place at home, with Imogen and Kate around. We walked in Highgate woods, along the paths laden with cow's parsley and flowering white hawthorn, and had tea in the café. I'd made a chicken casserole for supper. He was very good with the girls, and showed great interest in Kate's Anne Frank project and Imogen's psychology studies.

On Saturday morning, I'd booked us all on the London Eye. I was actually terrified of heights, but we'd never been, and it would give Marius a good view of the city. We then lunched at The Oxo Tower – a venue so beyond my budget that I'd never been there before, but it was a huge treat. Afterwards, we passed a couple of hours at Tate Modern, just to inject a bit of culture. Marius was surprisingly knowledgeable about modern art.

On Sunday the girls had revision to do, so I drove us up to Cambridge, with the idea of punting on the Cam and a picnic. Although nearly mid-May, the weather was cool, and I wasn't able to wear the floaty Liberty dress I'd imagined I would.

Being a man, Marius insisted on giving punting a go, but he struggled. He didn't quite lose the pole – although nearly – and progress was slow, but amusing. It would have taken us all day to get to Grantchester, as planned, so we stopped at a landing stage in the backs and had our picnic in a field amongst cow pats and some over-inquisitive brown cows. I'd bought some rather good cheeses, salami and paté from the extortionately expensive deli in Highgate, a French loaf, grapes and a bottle of Chablis.

"Have you ever had a grape peeled for you?" Marius asked, as he popped one into my mouth.

"I don't believe I have." He stroked my hair.

"I've thought about you constantly, Leo – and you?"

"Of course, but I'm rather new at this dating game."

"Then we can both learn to play the game together."

He reclined and drew me towards him and we had our first kiss. It felt good and I wanted more.

"I won't rush you into anything, Leo," he said, "but I can't tell you how happy you make me feel. Next time you visit Holland we'll go to the Kleine Vuurtoren for a few days, just the two of us. How does that sound?"

"Maybe over the girls' half term in a fortnight? They can go to Scotland to stay with Russell."

Everything to do with Marius seemed to happen fortnightly, so two weeks later I found myself at Rotterdam airport, which is only an hour's drive to the Kleine Vuurtoren. He was waiting for me in Arrivals with a huge bunch of tulips. We hugged. I was very excited to see more of Holland, and we drove through the extensive docks into flat, cultivated countryside – with windmills, dykes and gabled red brick houses, all with neatly attended gardens. The state-of-the-art bridges spanning the two crossings to his island were incredible. Marius told me that the Dutch are famed for their engineering – dykes, roads, bridges, airports. And that they'd made embankments, low walls and other systems around New York to prevent the city from flooding.

"The Kleine Vuurtoren is a play on words, Leo: 'kleine' being small, and 'light house' being as the design of the house is full of light."

The large bungalow was in the last street of Nieuw Haamstede before the dunes, in the shadow of a magnificent red and white striped lighthouse – like a huge barber's pole. Always keen to provide me with information, he told me it was built in 1837, standing forty-seven metres high, and one of the tallest lighthouses in Holland.

The Kleine Vuurtoren was light and fresh, constructed mainly of glass, with cool, tiled flooring throughout. It was like nowhere I'd ever been, but I was more concerned with the sleeping arrangements, which was all I could think about. His housekeeper had left a coffee tray and home-made biscuits out for us. Everything was perfectly organised, but rather sterile.

"This is a beautiful place, Marius," I said as we drank our coffee on a paved terrace by the covered swimming pool. "I can see why this is your escape from the city."

"Thank you, Leo. My parents had a lot of objection from neighbours when they built the house in 1986 in view of its avant-garde design, but my father was an architect and it wasn't long before many of the other houses in the street were demolished and re-built in the same style. It was his retirement project, and they lived here for a very happy twenty-four years. Now, I expect you want to freshen up."

I followed him along a corridor.

"I've given you this room, with your own bathroom, and I'm just along there on the right."

"We're still learning how to play the game, aren't we?!"

After he'd put my luggage down on the rack we kissed and I started to feel more relaxed, with the prospect of my own bathroom. Strange how your priorities change when you are middle-aged: there are things that one doesn't wish to share with a relative stranger, bathroom-wise, and this alleviated a major concern.

A seafood platter was in the fridge for our lunch: smoked salmon, lobster, pickled herrings, with fresh bread and fruit.

After lunch, we walked hand-in-hand through the dunes for ten minutes before reaching the sea. The white, sandy beach was endless – and the tide far out. It was breathtakingly beautiful. How could I possibly not fall in love with Marius, with everything he had to offer? By comparison, it made my life in Highgate seem utterly suburban and pedestrian. I could see myself entertaining friends from London at the Kleine Vuurtoren, who would be massively impressed.

When we got back, I asked Marius if I could have a bath before we went out for dinner.

"I'll run it for you now, Leo," he offered.

A foaming, deep bubble bath awaited me, and a flute of cold champagne on a wooden stool. I was 'travelling first class', as my late father used to say. I lingered in the bath. We dined in Domburg, on the neighbouring south island, in a bustling street café, with mainly English and German fellow diners. I hadn't much appetite as the seafood lunch had been filling, but ordered a small portion of *mosselen* and frites. I was given a plastic apron/bib to wear. The Dutch are so practical. Marius had *biefstuk* and frites.

"You certainly know how to look after your guests, Marius," I said, trying to eat the mussels as politely as possible.

"That's my business, Leo: hospitality."

"And will I find a little bottle of perfume on my pillow tonight?" I joked.

"You'll find a large bottle of perfume on my pillow!" he replied.

There was no bottle of perfume on his pillow, but I did lay my head on it as he carefully seduced me and we made love for the first time. I felt like a vestal virgin, in the words of Procol Harum's 'Lighter Shade of Pale'. It was gentle and considerate, but not fuelled by passion and desire, like in my youth. Maybe that had something to do with me, as I was approaching 'the change'. We then slept until I had to wake him urgently to ask where his bathroom was. It seemed that the mussels had disagreed with me big time, and all my private toileting anxieties went out the window as the rotten mussel travelled through me, like molten lead. I must have been in there for a good ten minutes before I found Marius in the sitting room on his computer.

"My poor love. I'm so sorry." he said. He wrapped a cashmere blanket over my shoulders, and poured me a glass of iced water.

"Maybe you'd feel happier in your own room tonight, with your own bathroom. Sleep as long as you want tomorrow, and I'll put your electric blanket on." Marius couldn't have been more considerate.

My night was troubled only once more, but I still felt rather weak and depleted when I woke, late on Saturday. We didn't go sailing, as planned, but instead went to a café to watch the gliders on the airstrip in Haamstede. Marius wanted lunch at The Torenhoeve, a charming little hotel next to the lighthouse, before another walk to the beach. It was a lovely weekend, but marred by the unfortunate meal. On the drive back to Rotterdam on Sunday afternoon, Marius tempted me with some information:

"I've a big, new and exciting project on, Leo, but I don't want to jinx things by telling you just now. I so much want you to be part of it, and when things are completed, you'll be the first to know."

This stirred my interest in Holland, and Marius, even more.

PART 2

I moved to Amsterdam to live with Marius in the autumn of 2017, when Kate started at Oxford. We'd spent a lot of time together in the intervening years, and our relationship had been steady and sure. I knew he loved me. Naturally, we'd discussed marriage, but both came to the same conclusion of 'once bitten, twice shy', so there was no point; we were happy as we were.

His project was to buy and convert a large house of students' accommodation, next to the Indrapura restaurant on Rembrandtplein, into a chic eight-bedroomed boutique hotel, which he'd named 'The Hotel Leonora'. It was much smaller than The Galilei, and he'd kept the top floor for our own apartment, with a large roof terrace. The Leonora was probably the most exclusive and expensive boutique hotel in Amsterdam, and had been fitted to the highest standards: all the furniture, lamps and rugs from OKA, bedding from The White Company, top quality memory-foam mattresses, complimentary perfume and bathroom dispensers from Jo Malone, and all glass, crockery and cutlery from Villeroy & Boch. It took me nearly a year to source everything, which was great fun.

The bedroom ceilings were high enough to accommodate canopied or four-poster beds, which are always a luxury. Like The Galilei, there was only a breakfast room, small lounge and bar, but the room service snacks were of the highest quality. I took over doing the flowers for both hotels, and our lives were busy and fulfilled, but with not much time for socialising or visiting The Kleine Vuurtoren. It was hard work, but seemed to be paying off, and we were constantly fully-booked.

I saw the girls every couple of months – either by going back to Highgate for the odd week, or them visiting us. The husband of my friend, Collette, had gone bankrupt, and they'd been forced to sell their house in Hampstead, so it suited me well that they were living in my house, paying a small rent and keeping an eye on things. Our guests at The Leonora were mainly Scandinavian and Japanese tourists. It was Imogen who spotted an opportunity to provide them with a tailored guests' package for sightseeing the city and visiting places of interest within an hour's drive. After graduating from Aberdeen, she'd got a job teaching psychology at her old school, which she tired of after six months; she just felt it wasn't going anywhere. So she joined us. In the evenings, she taught herself Dutch through an intensive Rosetta Stone language course, in conjunction with learning through the Dutch Babbel App. With the help of her German G.C.S.E, she was fluent within three months, and moved out to Amsterdam to live in Marius's old flat in the summer of 2018. We bought a customised minibus, advertising The Leonora, which she used to drive our guests around and to take them for longer excursions to Haarlem, The Lisse Gardens and The Keukenhof, The Hague and the coastal town of Scheveningen. Kate came to help out in her holidays, and when Marius's son Kees graduated from university he worked at The Leonora before becoming manager of The Galilei. It was a real family business, and I felt truly blessed with my lot.

In February 2019, some English guests checked in: Kit and Alex Dalrymple. Unusually, we were having a drink at the bar after an exhausting day spent with landscape gardeners on our roof terrace. It was our final project. So as not to be too disruptive to our guests, the men had arrived at five in the morning to take plants, pots and paving stones up in the service lift. I filled the terracotta containers with soil and compost, and got to work with planting, while Marius oversaw deliveries of garden furniture and the laying of the patio. Like an Alan Titchmarsh garden make-over, the whole area was transformed in a day. The Dalrymples came into the bar and ordered gin and tonics. We were the only ones there.

"Please," said Marius, "do come and join us. Marius and Leo van den Berg. We hope you're enjoying your stay and that you've everything you need? We don't normally have a drink in our hotel, but tonight we're celebrating the completion of our roof garden. We're going to have a bottle of champagne. Are you here for business or pleasure?"

"Business mostly," Kit replied. "In two months I'll take up my post as the new curator of seventeenth century Dutch painting at The Rijksmuseum. As I'm sure you know, it has the best collection of Dutch art from the Middle Ages to the present day. I'll be responsible for organising exhibitions and research projects. I was actually appointed two years ago."

"How fascinating," I said. "Is it unusual for an Englishman – or should I say a Scotsman – to take such an important job?"

"They've never appointed one before, as far as I know, but it seems they liked my qualifications."

"Which are?" Marius asked. I sensed a bit of friction between the men.

"After studying art history in London and getting a Master's Degree, I worked for the Courtauld Institute of Art as Deputy Director. It's London's centre for the study of art history. I then went on to curate The Burrell Collection in Glasgow, specialising in late medieval and early Renaissance European Art. The Centre closed for refurbishment in late 2016, and is not due to re-open until 2021. So, since 2017 I've been lecturing at The Courtauld Institute, and am involved with various other research and restoration projects. My experience is very broad, but no one can surpass The Dutch Masters, in my opinion. I'm very excited about my new job, but Alex isn't sure about relocating to Holland, making friends, and so on – are you, darling?"

Alex had a cut-glass Cheltenham Ladies College accent. "To be honest, it will be a big challenge for me, with Kit so busy, and I don't know a soul in Holland, or anything about Dutch culture."

"I'm still a relative new-comer at this game, Alex, but everyone's so friendly here, and I can help you get familiarised with things. My ex-husband lives in Glasgow, Kit, Russell Johnson. Have you ever come across him, or his partner Martin Black?"

Kit cleared his throat. "I don't know any gay people," was his dour reply, before continuing, "The main purpose of this visit is to find rented accommodation. My employers will help us with the rent, so we're looking for an up-market and central apartment, preferably with three bedrooms."

Marius saw an opportunity. "I've a beautiful flat on Spui, which would be perfect for you, and very central. Only two bedrooms, but it's large and spacious, at just under a hundred square metres. At the moment, Leo's daughter lives there, but we can easily make alternative arrangements for her. Would you like us to show you around tomorrow?"

"That would be very kind, Marius, thank you," Kit said. "And might you be able to recommend a nearby restaurant for dinner? We've had a long day and we're hungry."

"We're going to eat at the Indonesian restaurant next door, The Indrapura," Marius said. "Do please join us. It's traditional cuisine from The Dutch East Indies, part of our heritage, and the best one in town."

The invitation was accepted, and we dined at our usual table. Marius suggested that he order all the food.

"It's a good article you have in Easy Jet's in-flight magazine," Alex remarked, over our starters.

"Yes, my daughter, Kate, organised that. She has a friend who does marketing for Easy Jet. We invited one of their travel writers here for a night and gave her the works. She was researching Europe's best twelve boutique hotels, and it seems we made it in. It's not exactly Concorde in-flight reading, but any publicity's good, and it's brought us clientele. Do you work, Alex?"

"Yes, I'm a nutritionist. I started off with a private business, treating people with weight and dietary issues, but now I specialise in calorie-counting meals for restaurant menus. It's becoming very popular in London, and important to help those with diabetes, obesity and other weight-related conditions. And the young are keen to know their calorie counts. I also act as a consultant for various companies, advising on their canteens and meal calorie contents. It's important to keep employees healthy."

"That's really interesting. There would certainly be a market for that here, with so many food outlets," I replied.

"Would I need to learn Dutch?"

"No," I assured her. Everyone speaks English here."

Alex wasn't that slim herself, but certainly not overweight.

"I'd be interested to know what countries have the healthiest diets?" I asked her.

"I'd say Iceland, Japan, Switzerland, Israel and Norway. Of course, the basic Mediterranean diet is a healthy one, but without all the pizza and pasta!"

"I don't think the basic Dutch diet is that healthy – we love our fried food, potatoes, meat and cheese," Marius said, "and I hate to think how many calories there are in a Rijsttafel!"

"A lot, I would say, but who's counting tonight?" Alex replied, her mouth full of spicy shredded beef in fried chilli and coconut. "Everything's absolutely delicious."

Kit was quieter, but Alex had something about her that made you want to be her friend – a sort of detached classiness. I warmed to her. Her prematurely (or maybe intentional) grey hair was immaculately cut in a long bob, and her eyes were very dark brown. I guessed she might be a couple of years older than me.

The evening was a great success and we arranged to meet the following morning. I rang Imogen to make sure everything in the flat was clean and tidy, and suggested she buy some flowers.

Marius got up early to check out prices of similar flat rentals, so as to quote Kit and Alex a competitive price.

They were still having breakfast when we came down.

"I hope you're not calorie-counting, Alex?" I said. "Steer well clear of the *appelstroop*, the hazelnut-chocolate spread, Hagelslag chocolate sprinkles and the *stroopwafels*!" It seemed that food was going to be a good talking point.

We took a taxi to Spui, with Marius providing local information:

"Spui is a popular and historic area. The main square was originally a body of water, forming the southern limit of the city until the early fifteenth century, when the Singel canal was dug as an outer moat around the centre. The Amsterdam Museum's here, and also the Begijnhof – a group of historic buildings surrounding a Medieval courtyard. There are some interesting sculptures around too."

Imogen was out, and had left the flat spotless, with two beautiful flower arrangements.

They seemed to like it, but were keen to overlook a canal, and to have an extra bedroom. Marius mentally lowered the price. "You'll find canal-side properties more expensive, and noisier, but of course you must do your research before reaching a decision."

"May we take you out for coffee?" Kit asked us.

Marius was, as always, intent on keeping control. "That sounds a lovely idea, but my flagship hotel is only around the corner, on Singel, so why don't we go there?"

"Gosh – two hotels! You must be so busy," Alex said.

"We have very good and reliable staff. In fact, my son has recently taken over as Manager of The Galilei," Marius informed them.

Whilst he ordered our coffees, I showed Alex the fish tank, and told her about the little yellow fish with behavioural problems – who had long since died of exhaustion!

"Kit loves fishing. His family have an estate near Perth and he's fished there since he was a boy; fly-fishing, that is. Sadly, he's the second son, so it was his brother who recently inherited the estate. Kit wasn't that interested, but I'd have loved it."

"There's wonderful fishing on the Veerse Meer, a lagoon where Marius keeps his yacht," I replied. "Maybe we could take you there one day."

"Kit would really love that. Thank you."

We'd been intending to go to the Kleine Vuurtoren for Saturday and Sunday night, but decided to remain in town whilst the Dalrymples were staying. Instead, we went to the Saturday flea market on Waterlooplein, which sometimes had an outdoor furniture reclamation stall. We were lucky to find a terracotta lion's head wall fountain, complete with spout and trough, which was perfect for our seating area on the roof terrace. Also, a stone chapel-arched triptych mirror. Marius went to get the minibus, while I had a browse. I found myself thinking about Alex, and wondered what they were doing. I hoped we'd become good friends; she might fill a gap in my life.

Marius went to look for help to get the fountain and mirror up to the roof terrace, whilst I had a cup of tea in the lounge, hoping that Kit and Alex would return. If they took the apartment it would be a neat way to keep in close touch.

I cooked us spaghetti carbonara for supper, and drank half a bottle of Merlot in fifteen minutes. Marius was doing a shift in reception in the hope of seeing the Dalrymples, who didn't materialise.

"What rental price did you quote Kit?" I asked him, as he was opening another bottle.

"Seventeen hundred euros a month, with electricity and water on top. They won't find anything better than that on Spui. There's something about that man which I dislike, and I don't trust him."

"Imogen will have to move in with us if they do take it. For the time-being anyway. But what if they want to live nearer the Rijksmuseum?"

"It's not such a good residential area. Kit's got to think about Alex. Do you mind if we don't talk about it now? I'm tired."

I could sense that Marius was in a strange mood.

"Is anything the matter?" I asked him. "You seem a bit agitated."

"Not really. It's just that I thought you were a bit over-friendly with Alex today, and this is a business matter. They're our guests, not our friends, and also possible tenants of my apartment."

"You were keen to make a friend of me, when I was a guest at The Galilei," I reminded him.

"That was different. You were on your own and seemed a bit lost, and I fancied you."

I decided not to reply, so remained quiet until I re-visited the subject after supper, when we were watching TV. Fuelled by alcohol, I wanted to provoke an argument:

"I'm sick of Dutch television, and Dutch everything. It's all about you, Marius. You, you, you. Meeting Alex made me realise that I need my own space and my own friend. What's wrong with that?"

"Oh for God's sake, Leo. This is business, and it shouldn't be mixed with pleasure. Join a club if you want to make your own friends. I'm going to bed."

In a second relationship, there comes a moment when you wonder what the other side of the story was in the previous one, and it was beginning to occur to me that Marius was so focused on his own and the hotel's success that I was becoming marginalised – possibly like his first wife. 'Leopards don't change their spots,' I thought as I opened another bottle and went to bed in the spare room at one in the morning.

I had a fearful hangover on Sunday. Marius was nowhere to be seen, but I found him serving breakfast to Kit and Alex. It seemed they had viewed another four flats, and come to the conclusion that the three-bedroomed ones had smaller rooms, so they wanted to take Marius's.

"That's great news." said Marius. "Would you like to have drinks with us in our apartment upstairs this evening, so we can discuss things? And if you don't have any other plans for today, maybe you'd like to visit Scheveningen, a pretty seaside town, and have a delicious seafood lunch and a walk on the beach? It's only a fifty-minute drive, and Imogen could take you in the hotel minibus."

Both arrangements were agreed on, and they came up for drinks with us at six thirty.

Kit had laid a tray with a bottle of Sauvignon, some chorizo, cubes of Leerdammer and spicy pimento peppers.

"You've an interesting art collection," Kit observed. "Where did you get those screen-prints of Chairman Mao from?"

"Fabulous, aren't they? I inherited them from my late uncle, about ten years ago," Marius replied. "He lived in New York and was a friend of Andy Warhol's."

"Really. It's possible they're stolen property. Were you aware of that?"

"Stolen?" Marius paled.

Kit was warming to his subject. "I act as a Consultant to The Art Register, the world's largest database of stolen art. I mostly value Old Masters from private collections, a lot of which have out-of-date valuations. I'll have to check the colour-ways, but the timing fits with two Mao screen-prints and two Campbell Soup ones, which were stolen from a private collection in The Hague. Can you provide Provenance and proof of purchase? They would be valued today at about a hundred thousand pounds, which isn't a huge amount in terms of stolen art treasures. But as they're so iconic, I remember them, and as far as I know they haven't been found. Only a very small percentage of art napping is recovered – between five and ten percent. Receiving stolen art carries a heavy penalty." He took several photos on his phone.

"This is a serious allegation, Kit," I said, feeling the blood drain through my veins.

"Indeed, but I'm only doing my job, Leo. I'll be looking into it, and it may be that my position would be jeopardised if we rent your flat. I'm sure you understand."

No rental details were discussed, and Kit and Alex left. We sat in silence for several minutes before I attempted to give Marius the Spanish Inquisition:

"Well, that was fun. Were you aware that you might be in receipt of stolen goods?"

"Of course not. I'm going out."

"Fine."

There were now severe cracks in our relationship, not least being that I might lose Alex, who I'd only just met, but latched on to. I sobbed into another bottle of Sauvignon, and went to bed without supper or taking my make-up off. I felt totally lost and humiliated, and couldn't give a flying fuck where Marius had gone.

The next morning, when making coffee and still in my dressing gown, I noticed that the two Campbell's Soup screen-prints had been taken down in the kitchen. My heart sank. Moments later I heard keys in the front door. Marius appeared with Kit and Alex. I apologised for my appearance, and made coffee. The atmosphere between us had changed, but Marius was seemingly calm.

"Marius," Kit said authoritatively, "my photos have proved that your prints are stolen property. You have legal rights to get a full refund of the purchase price from the seller, but the police need to be informed. You may still be charged with handling stolen goods, which is illegal, but not if you bought them unknowingly."

Marius took a deep breath: "Okay. I bought the prints from a French guy called Antoine, who I met at a gallery opening. He offered me a good price of thirty thousand euros, and told me he'd inherited them from his late uncle in New York. I don't have any contact details for him – he just delivered the prints to my flat for cash. That's all I know, but I can probably provide bank details of the cash withdrawal."

"Thirty thousand euros was quite a lot on the black market for those prints ten years ago. You didn't buy the Campbell's Soup ones as well then?"

"No. Absolutely not."

"So, why weren't you truthful to me yesterday?" Kit continued to interrogate Marius.

"Come on. I believed the guy. I'm not into stolen art, I can assure you. I've a good reputation in Amsterdam and am well-respected." Kit ignored his remark.

"And where was the gallery where you met him?"

"On Prinsengracht. Galleries tend to be closed on Mondays, but we could visit it now, if you like."

Marius and Kit took a taxi to Prinsengracht, while Alex stayed with me.

"I'm so sorry about all this, Leo," she said, putting her hand on my arm. "It must be awful for you. Are you okay? You look as if you've been crying."

"Oh, God. I don't know where to start. Life hasn't been that easy with Marius for the past year or two. It's been so much hard work getting The Leonora up and running. I thought he was perfect, but then no one is. Men. I'll probably go back to London for a bit of breathing space as soon as I can get a flight."

"Maybe we could meet up?" Alex suggested. "We live in Pimlico."

"I'd really like that."

"Kit also buries himself in work, and he didn't want children as he thought they'd interfere with his career. Amsterdam was going to be a new beginning for us, but it hasn't got off to a very good start. He's not the easiest person either. And you've both been so kind."

We exchanged phone numbers and gave each other a hug.

Alex went down to pack and I had a bath and then went to look for the Campbell's Soup prints, which I found underneath the spare room bed. I went down to give them to Kit. That would surely be the final nail in the coffin, but I didn't care. Marius returned an hour later in a foul mood.

"Was the gallery open?" I asked him.

"No, but Kit will be following things up with them."

"Why did you lie to me, Marius? I don't like being lied to. I'm going back to London for a week or so to give us some breathing space. I'll stay with Imogen tonight."

Marius put his head between his hands on the kitchen table, but I felt no sympathy.

I booked my flight for the following morning.

Back home, I reflected on my reflex action to give the Soup prints back to Kit, and wondered what would implode in my absence. I slightly regretted my hasty decision. Fortunately, Colette and David were happy for me to stay with them in my house, but that wasn't the same either – they were incredibly untidy and always cooking food with garlic. The cooker was filthy and covered in what looked like congealed dahl. I felt just as trapped as I'd done in Holland, with no say in things, so I called Alex and invited her up to Highgate. We met at the tube station and walked through the woods, before having lunch in the café. I asked her about the Soup prints.

"Kit arranged for them to be returned to the house in The Hague, along with the Mao prints, which he recovered from your flat."

"And what will the consequences be?" I asked her.

"I don't know. You'd have to speak to Kit about that."

"I feel disloyal, hurt, angry and confused, Alex."

"I understand, Leo. Who could have foreseen all this?"

"After Russell left me for Martin, my life went into a slump. He moved on to a new relationship and I was left behind in Highgate to raise Imogen and Kate. I became suspicious of men and lost my confidence. Marius seemed to fill all those gaps and offered me a new start in a new country. I put my whole life on hold to move to Amsterdam, and lost touch with many of my friends. Now I don't know what the future holds. I was never in love with him, but he seemed a good bet, and so solid. Plus, I liked what he had to offer me, and the lifestyle. Now he's left me in a sort of mental, physical and emotional abyss." I started crying. Alex took my hand.

Being a Cancerian, I hate conflict and arguments, so I spent a few days just walking aimlessly round Highgate, trying to decide what I wanted to do, and thinking a great deal about Alex, who I was starting to feel seriously attracted to – in a spiritual kind of way. We were in similar predicaments, which may explain why I was so drawn to her. My life was in a complete mess, and not for the first time.

Marius rang me on Thursday. He sounded calm.

"You were right to return the Soup prints to Kit, Leo. I couldn't have lived with them. I'm so sorry for lying and embarrassing you. It seems that the Gallery has no record of an Antoine on their database, and all the prints have been returned to The Hague. I really didn't know they were stolen, and thankfully the police aren't going to make any charges against me. Somehow the story has leaked into the Dutch press – I suspect through Kit – to make himself a good name before starting his new job. I need your support, Leo. Please come back. The Dalrymples aren't going to take Spui, so you can always stay there with Imogen until we've sorted things out between us. We could go to the Kleine Vuurtoren this weekend, if you like."

This was a reasonable suggestion, and I couldn't think of a better alternative, so I took the ferry from Harwich to the Hoek of Holland the following day to give myself a bit more time. Thoughts about Alex moving to Amsterdam filled me with a delicious, secret warmth, and I wished she was standing next to me, watching the churning frothy wake at the stern of the ship.

Marius met me with a huge bunch of daffodils. As both of us were non-confrontational, we didn't talk much on the drive to Haamstede, but Marius said he didn't want us to have anything more to do with the Dalrymples. I got the feeling that his dislike of Kit was because he sensed they were similar. He told me that despite the adverse publicity, The Leonora had had a busy week, with Imogen doing the flowers for both hotels.

I slept in the spare room, and Marius woke me with breakfast in bed on Saturday morning.

"I've been thinking, Leo. As I wasn't fined for having possession of the prints, and we have wall space to fill, let's go to Zierikzee today. They've lots of galleries there, and good restaurants.

Zierikzee is a charming little port, bustling with life, and it took our minds off things. We bought a huge, modern pastel seascape and a bronze resin sculpture of a whale tail on a marble plinth. Also, two contemporary still life oils of aubergines and artichokes for the kitchen.

The next six weeks passed without incident. Alex and I spoke and e-mailed quite often, and I continued to think about her a great deal. They arrived during the last week of March to settle into their duplex canal-side apartment on Keizersgracht, very close to Marius's flat.

"I so wanted to live on a barge, but of course got over-ridden by Kit. He said they're not secure," Alex said as we were having our first coffee together. "It's been so stressful, packing up and deciding what and what not to bring. I nearly didn't come, were it not for you being here."

"I'm so pleased you did."

We arranged to visit Lisse and the Keukenhof Gardens later in the week, and I collected Alex from the café on Friday. I'd told Marius that The Keukenhof had a flower-arranging demonstration day and that I needed some fresh ideas. Although slightly early, the tulip fields were advanced because of the warm weather, and Alex was bowled over by the colours and the Gardens. We lunched at the same Heineken café, where I'd been with Marius (but steered away from the croquettes), and shared a bottle of rosé, and then another. I wasn't aware of drink-driving laws in Holland, but got away with it. Feeling elated after such a happy day, and in the mood for more wine, I opened a bottle as soon as I got home. By the time Marius got in I was asleep on the sofa, not having prepared supper.

"You're drunk, Leo. Have you really been to Lisse?" he asked me.

"Yes, but I decided to stop at a bar overlooking the tulip fields as it was such a lovely evening. Is that alright? For God's sake get off my case." Marius just shook his head and went out to get us takeaway pizzas.

Over supper I provokingly suggested that my friends, the Hampsons, might make use of the Kleine Vuurtoren for a week's holiday at mates' rates. I could so do with some new company.

"They don't have much money, and a teenage son with cerebral palsy. He's my godson, actually."

"I wouldn't want strangers staying there, Leo."

"They're not strangers, they're my friends. Anna and I were at boarding school. They're lovely. Maybe I could join them?"

"I couldn't do without you for a whole week, Leo, so the answer is no."

Another brick wall, and I was then really in the mood to push for an argument.

"It's been pissing me off for a while that all our socialising is with the hotel's guests. It's so transitory and unrewarding. We've no real friends, Marius. Everything focuses around you and the hotel and I feel lonely."

"You just don't get it. This is the hotel business, Leo. We're hosts and it makes us a lot of money. Stop complaining, and why don't you join an evening class, like I've suggested before. Learn a new hobby – painting maybe?"

"Don't patronise me. I'm not a child wanting an activity class after school. I'd like us to make friends, like normal people do. Take them to the Kleine Vuurtoren – you at least used to do that with Cornie – go out to dinner, maybe even go on holiday with. If we're making all this money, why can't we go away to somewhere hot and tropical, just to get away?"

"Maybe we could have a city break then."

I gave up at that point.

Over the next couple of months Alex and I had some wonderful trips: visiting The Hague to go to The Binnenhof and The International Courts of Justice, to Haarlem to listen to an organ recital in The Grote Kerk, to Scheveningen for seafood lunches and walks on the beach. We even went to the Sex Museum, which was a good laugh, although we were the oldest visitors by far. We met frequently for coffee or lunch, visited the markets, and went to free lunchtime recitals in The Opera House. In order to facilitate time together, I joined a gym, with no intention of ever using it. I also bought some expensive gym kit, which I regularly put in the laundry basket, washed and hung out. It was surprisingly easy to be deceitful, and I was becoming rather good at it, although I don't think that Alex had any idea about my growing feelings for her. On our excursions out of town, we always took the train so that Marius couldn't check the mileage on his car.

The café we frequented asked Alex to do a calorie-count on their cake menu, as did The Lotus Flower – the most expensive Japanese eaterie in Amsterdam. Also 'Dill', a Scandinavian smorgasbord restaurant, wanted a full calorie-count on their menu, and they asked me to do a weekly flower arrangement. I told Marius about this with great excitement, over a cup of tea, after I'd had a lovely day out with Alex to Haarlem for an afternoon organ recital. I told him I'd been to the gym. His reply really put the dampeners down on me.

"Leo. You don't have time for extra flower-arranging. The Leonora is one of the top ten boutique hotels in Europe and you have to give it your full attention."

"I want to earn some of my own money and to have a focus outside the hotel. You're so controlling. I don't have any freedom, and need to reclaim my self-respect."

"Fine," he said, and that was the end of the conversation.

In early June, Marius told me that he and Kees would be going to Utrecht to attend an Elite Hotel Management Course for the weekend, staying over on the Saturday night. I didn't have long to plan, but Alex and I decided to go to Terschelling, an island belonging to the province of North Holland, for the weekend. I'd been stashing away euros for such an eventuality, and Alex hired a car for us, which I drove. Everything was covered.

Terschelling, the first island off the north mainland, was somewhere I'd never been to with Marius. It was unbelievably stunning – the azure sea, endless beaches and dunes, and very under-populated. I'd booked us into a two-bedroomed waterside log cabin, and paid cash on our arrival. Alex had bought a bottle of champagne, wine, and a lasagne for our supper. As we ate crayfish and frites for lunch at an outdoor seafood café overlooking a marina, I told Alex that I'd never been so happy in my life:

"I feel so free when I'm with you, Alex. You allow me to be myself. I don't feel controlled by you."

"Me too. Kit's also controlling, but he's pleased we have a good friendship. He likes you."

I'd never told Alex that Marius had pretty much forbidden me to have anything to do with her, nor that he detested her homophobic husband.

After a long walk along a deserted beach, we checked into our cabin at tea time. I opened the bottle of champagne and we changed into our bikinis, spending a couple of hours in the jacuzzi, laughing and telling stories about our youth. I hadn't been so carefree, or had so much fun, since I was a child. It was a wonderful weekend, but went by far too quickly.

I made sure that I was home in good time and had pre-prepared a fish pie for Sunday's supper – Marius's favourite. I could sense that he was in a tetchy mood when he got in, just after six.

"How was your seminar?" I asked him brightly.

"Fine. And your weekend?"

"Was lovely and quiet. I went to the flower market yesterday to get bulbs, and then shopped for Kate's birthday presents. Today I did some planting on the roof terrace."

"Anything else?"

"No, not really."

"So how did you find the time to go to Terschelling?" he enquired.

"Sorry."

"To Terschelling, like I said. That's where you've been since Saturday morning. Yes?"

"Of course, I haven't been to Terschelling. I don't even know where it is. What on earth gave you that idea?"

"Because I now have a tracker on your mobile phone since I don't trust you. I know you don't go to that gym either."

"How dare you interfere with my private life? I don't interfere with yours," I virtually spat at him.

"Who were you with. Was it Kit?"

"For God's sake, Marius. I have a secret life because of you. I count for nothing. This is all a déjà vu of your marriage to Cornelia."

"You lied to me, Leo."

"Yes, but you've lied to me too."

"But not about something personal."

"A lie is a lie, Marius. You make your own rules, but my trust in you is broken."

"Get out," he shouted, "and don't come back."

I packed a small bag and went to his flat. Imogen was giving a dinner party, and I explained that we'd had a row and went to bed with a bottle of wine. I texted Alex to say I needed to see her urgently at our café in the morning. I hardly slept that night, and my time in Amsterdam was running out. I needed to do some plain speaking to Alex. I'd nothing to lose.

We met at eleven on Monday morning at our café .

"Marius has had a tracker fitted on my phone, and he knows I went to Terschelling for the weekend, but not who with. My life's in tatters, Alex. I've nothing to lose other than to say that I love your company, and want to be with you. I'm not a lesbian and this is isn't sexual, but I feel we could live happily together, with our own freedom. I'm sorry to blurt all this out. I hope I haven't embarrassed you."

"You've read my mind, Leo."

"I need to have a place in London for Imogen and Kate, but can sell my house in Highgate and maybe buy us a narrow boat in Little Venice, seeing as we both love the water."

MR WRIGHT 2018

It wasn't exactly internet dating. I'd mis-sent a text meant for my neighbour, who'd given me a cucumber over the fence. I thought I'd thank her, but must have got a digit wrong. The reply came back immediately.

"I haven't given you a cucumber, but would like to!"

"You sound fun," I replied, slightly fuelled by having a few lagers at the pub with my friend, Angie. We were both single and trying to find a partner. Angie had given internet dating a go, but was always disappointed, so she didn't recommend it.

"They aren't who they say they are," she said, "and never go by a photograph," but this opportunity seemed like it was meant to be.

"Where do you live?" came his (I assumed) quick reply.

"Chelmsford. You?"

"Brighton."

"What do you do?"

"A radio technician. You?"

I had to think quickly, as didn't want to say I was a cleaner.

"I'm a psychic medium."

"Cool. Did you predict you'd meet a handsome stranger?"

"No. It's hard to predict for myself."

"Well, this is your lucky night. What's your name?"

"Candy. Yours?"

"Owen Wright."

"Is that your real name?"

"Yes. I'm Welsh, and I'm looking for love. How old are you?"

"Thirty. You?"

"Thirty two."

"Do you fancy meeting up sometime?" I boldly texted.

"Why not. I'll text you tomorrow as I have to help my mother now."

With what? I wondered – toileting/a bath/help with a jigsaw? It didn't sound very appealing. He obviously lived with his mother, and men who do that are generally rather immature, but it didn't put me off as he sounded fun. Also, if he was helping his mother, he must be a caring guy.

True to his word, Owen texted me in the morning. I'd got myself right worked up about the text exchanges, and had rung Angie to tell her.

"Be careful," she said. "Dating agencies offer some protection, but you're stepping into the unknown. He could be a mass murderer." I ignored her well-meant advice.

Owen and I agreed to meet at Brighton railway station the following Saturday morning. I trained up to Liverpool Street and then crossed London to Victoria. As I had to invent my psychic look, I'd bought a glittery caftan from TK Maxx, some strappy sandals and a sequin holdall. I'd lied to him, and hoped he hadn't lied to me, but the risk was exciting. I dabbed my wrists with Patchouli oil just as the train was drawing into the station. It wasn't exactly a red carnation job, but I guessed he'd recognise me by my outfit. He told me he'd be wearing a beige jacket, which sounded safe enough. My first impression, when I saw him at the barrier, was that he wasn't very tall, but not bad looking, with a stubbly beard and extremely tight black skinny jeans. It was difficult not to focus on the bulge in his crotch. He looked older than thirty two, and I think we were both a bit disappointed with each other's appearances.

"Well, hello," Owen said, "welcome to Brighton. I thought we'd go for a coffee and then play some mini-golf. We've two great little courses here – The Caveman and The Treetops."

"Okay," I said, "that sounds fun, but I've never done it before."

The frisson between us with the highly-charged exchanges of the cucumber texts had gone, and I was quite nervous. We went to Starbucks and sat outside so he could smoke his roll-ups. I wondered what the hell I had got myself into while he was getting our coffees: meeting a strange man to play mini-golf with in Brighton, and pretending to be a psychic medium. It was mad. I'd spent some time Googling psychics and how they recognised and developed their gift, so was reasonably confident of my subject. My cappuccino arrived with a chocolate heart on it.

"Have you ever done this before, Owen?" I asked him. "It's a little crazy!"

"I like crazy," he replied, "and the answer is no, I haven't."

"And you?"

"No. I've not done internet dating either."

"Nor me."

"So you live with your Mum?" I asked him.

"Yes. She got Parkinsons very early about five years ago and can't live alone any more as it's quite aggressive, but tell me about your psychic work. I'm really interested in that."

"Well. I realised that I had psychic tendencies as a child, but just thought I was a bit weird and different to the other kids. Then, when I left school, I bought a set of Tarot cards in a boot sale, and a book to study their meanings and relevance with other cards in a layout. I started doing readings for friends, who recommended me to theirs. My first job was as an assistant librarian, so there was plenty of time to study the occult and do readings in the evenings. I guess it just went on from there. My friend gave me a crystal ball, but I don't really use it. I rely on the Tarot cards and a person's aura." There was an element of truth in this spin because I do work in a library, but as a cleaner.

"Wow," he said. "And what does my aura tell you?"

"I can't just link in to you like that, Owen. I need to be in my own environment, with my cards, candles, joss-ticks and soft background music. Plus it's my day off today!"

"It would be great to have you, live, on our radio station."

I suddenly felt in deep water.

"I couldn't do 'live' readings on air, but maybe general predictions."

"Cool. I'll tell you about my job when we have lunch."

The mini-golf was hilarious, and a good ice-breaker, but rather difficult to play, with my caftan billowing in the Brighton breeze. Lunch was scampi and chips out of a newspaper-patterned box, eaten on a seafront bench. Owen had bought some Budweisers in his backpack.

"So, are you in the habit of texting strangers about cucumbers?" he asked me. I nearly choked with laughter, my mouth full of scampi and tartare sauce.

"That text was meant for my neighbour, who'd given me a cucumber. I must have got a digit wrong."

"Maybe it was divine destiny," he replied, "are you single?"

"Yes, just me and the cat. And you?"

"I was married, but it didn't work out."

"I'm sorry."

"No, don't be. My job's very rewarding, and Brighton's a great place to live. So vibrant."

We walked along the beach and had a cup of tea in a cafe. It was nearly five, so I thought I'd better be getting back as had my cleaning job to do in the early hours and needed to get to bed early.

"I'd better be heading off now, Owen. Got to feed the cat, but it's been a great day."

"I'm afraid I won't be able to visit you at home, Candy, because I'm allergic to cats, but I could come to Chelmsford." That was a relief, as I'd had worrying thoughts about needing to create a psychic parlour.

"I'd love to come down to Brighton again though," I said. Today's the first time I've ever been."

"You'd love The Lanes, with all the quirky little shops."

He walked me to the station, where we had a polite kiss and agreed that our next meeting would be in Chelmsford the following weekend. I called Angie on the train to tell her it had been a fun and safe day, and that he wasn't a weirdo. Also that he seemed to be a normal guy, with a good job in radio."

"Did you fancy him?" she asked.

"Not desperately, but I did like him. He was sparky."

"That's a good start."

Owen and I texted a few times during the week and he said he'd enjoyed our day out. I invested in some purple harem trousers and a floaty top to wear when we met the following Sunday at Chelmsford station. He was carrying a bunch of white rosebuds.

"I'm afraid there's not much to do in Chelmsford," I told him as we walked to the centre. "We could go bowling if you fancied an activity – or have lunch at the Everyman Cinema and watch a film. Do you have an Everyman in Brighton?"

"Of course. Brighton's a cultural hot spot, and they do good burgers there."

The film choices weren't great: 'The Lie', 'Mamma Mia, Here We Go Again', or 'The Favourite'. Owen wanted to see 'The Lie', but I told him I wasn't great on psychological thrillers as they were bad karma, so we settled for Abba, which was rather cheesy but uplifting. Afterwards we went to Wetherspoons and shared a bottle of red.

"Who looks after your Mum during the day and when you're at work?" I asked him.

"She's fine during the day, and has a call button."

"It must be a big strain on you," I said.

"Not really. She's only sixty-five and has all her marbles mentally. Also it helps me out as my wife's living in our flat until the divorce is finalised. "It's not a problem."

"Tell me about your work."

"I studied Media Production at Durham and got a job at Radio Reverb: a new cutting-edge Brighton radio station, right at their inception in 2004, although they weren't granted a broadcasting licence until 2007. I've worked there ever since. The job was pretty menial to begin with – doing the odd voice-over and sometimes giving a hand on the decks, but they soon realised I'd a flair for the technical side. Radio Reverb's a public analogue station, is non-profit making and advert-free. We deliver diverse radio to all ethnic groups in Brighton and Hove. It's firmly rooted in the community and offers free speech and diverse opinions. All our presenters are volunteers, and we provide a platform for local musicians, artists, writers and mental learning-awareness to a culturally diverse audience.

Sorry, I'm banging on now, but my job's so important to me."

"Wow. That sounds very high-brow." I calculated from this information that he could be nearer to thirty five.

"The work's voluntary, but I love it. We've actually been nominated for The National Diversity Awards in September, to be held in Liverpool, which is dead exciting."

There was a lull in the conversation, and Owen took a large swig of wine.

"I've been thinking. We've nowhere to meet, should we want to take things further, Candy. I live with my Mum, and you have a cat, but there is the possibility of spending a night together over the Awards weekend in a month's time, if you fancy it."

"Let's do it," I said.

My motive by then was entirely based on getting onto his radio station, but I could sacrifice myself for that. Fame at last! We agreed to meet in London the following weekend, and Owen said he'd find something fun for us to do.

I ordered *The Pocket Book on Tarot for Beginners* from Amazon for my handbag, and *The Tarot Revealed* by Paul Fenton-Smith: *A Simple Guide to Unlocking the Secrets of the Tarot.*

I clean at the library on Monday, Wednesday, Friday and Sunday nights from four to eight a.m. It brings me a salary of about a grand a month, which covers my basic expenses, and frees me up during the day. That night there was a note for me from the supervisor, saying that one of the cubicles in the men's toilets needed 'special attention'. Special attention was an understatement – it was in such a disgusting condition that I couldn't face cleaning it up. As it was only the fourth day of the month, I left my immediate resignation note for the supervisor and at that moment made the decision to become a medium. I borrowed a few books from the library, and in the morning went into a funky shop in town, Velvet Sunset, which sold joss-ticks, incense cones, essential oils, Tarot cards, angel cards, Bob Marley crocheted hats, lava lamps, disco balls, healing crystals, soothing music, gongs and so on. My research advised me to choose Tarot cards that I was attracted to, and which felt right, so I went for an old-fashioned, more traditional one: The Rider-Waite Tarot Deck, first printed in 1909. I also bought joss-ticks and holders, a lava lamp, scented candles, and CD's of 'The Sea', 'Mood Gongs' and 'Soft Pan Pipes'. I couldn't resist opening my cards in Pret-a-Manger, which was opposite Velvet Sunset. It was like falling in love – I felt elated, excited, happy and positive, and convinced that this was to be my new path in life, which Owen had given me.

I ordered a calorie-laden hot chocolate, topped with mini-marshmallows, squirty cream and cinnamon. Whilst examining the cards, a woman at the next table took an interest and asked me if I was a medium.

"I'm just starting out," I told her, "but if you'd like to help me with my first readings, I'd be delighted to use you as a guinea pig – obviously no charge."

"I'd really like that," she said. "I'm Elaine, and I live in Chelmsford."

"Don't tell me anything else about yourself, Elaine, but that would be a great help to me." We exchanged mobile numbers and I asked her to call me the following week.

On the bus ride home, I decided to turn my small spare room into a psychic parlour. Technically the room was my brother's, but he was in the Army and posted to Germany and had not yet spent a night there. We'd inherited the little house in Broomfield from our Nan, and I was so lucky not to have a mortgage and to have some spare cash. When I got home, I couldn't resist doing a simple three-card reading for myself. I shuffled the cards, which felt silky and energised, and then split them into three piles – the middle pile being the one to use. Just as I was about to draw my cards, Owen rang. I told him I was about to do a reading and would call him back.

My first card (which would be 'my' card) was The Queen of Cups, signifying intuition, imagination, creativity and action; a dreamer, whose vision is theirs. It stands for a muse and one who is deeply psychic. It's also a water sign card, and I'm Pisces. The cards implicated that if there is upheaval in the family or workplace, the outcome would be favourable. This was an encouraging start, particularly as I'd just lost myself my job.

My second card was The Knight of Pentacles, representing a person who is brave, and says that one coming into your life who will bring stability. It's a card of consolidation and of making moves towards concrete goals.

The final card I drew was The High Priestess, promising the unknown and, again, the development of psychic ability. Also, most importantly to me, that all knowledge she seeks comes from within. A time to plant the seeds of the future. These were the most brilliant and promising cards for my first reading and the start of my new stage in life. I knew the cards hadn't lied. Also, all my cards had been from the Major Arcana, which is unusual. I kissed the pack and rang Owen.

"Sorry, Owen, I was doing a reading when you rang."

"That's great – who for?"

"One of my regular clients."

"Cool. I just wondered if you fancied going to a live jazz concert at Kenwood House in North London this Sunday afternoon? It's great fun, outdoors, and we bring our own picnic. Starts at 2.30 p.m. Does that appeal? The artists are Ruben Hein,

The Simin Tander New Quartet, Michael Vare Kamp, The Jasper Blom Quarter and a jamming session with Carlo Nardozza and Philipps Thuriot. An amazing programme."

All this meant nothing to me, and I wasn't a great jazz fan, but was willing to embrace anything.

"Definitely. How about I bring the picnic and you the booze?"

"Fine. I'll bring a rug too. Dress warmly as it can be cold, sitting around."

We agreed to meet at the entrance gates at two.

Throughout the week I got myself more and more familiarised with my cards. I handled them often, and they gave off a warmth and energy. The net was full of helpful videos about layouts, interpretations and readings. I also learnt that you don't need to dress like a spooky psychic, as many of the on-line mediums wore normal clothes. Understanding the symbolism of the Major cards was just the beginning. The real power comes with using them with the four suits of the Minor Arcana: Cups, Swords, Wands and Pentacles, giving depth and direction when placed alongside the Majors. There was a lot to learn.

I went to a haberdasher in Moulsham Street to buy ready-made purple curtains, silver throws and black velvet for covering the surfaces, and set about painting the spare room lilac. I couldn't afford a new carpet, so bought a white shag-pile rug from the market. My parlour was ready for business!

Owen took my hand when we met on Sunday. He was wearing baggy shorts, and his legs were a little too hairy for my liking.

"No witchy gear on today, then?" he asked me, teasingly.

"No. I thought it might be cold."

The concert was great and vibrant. Owen told me that most

of the artists were Dutch, and part of Jazz Maastricht, which defines jazz as adventurous improvisation and communication between artist, audience and environment.

"We actually had Simin Tander on our station a few months ago. She's German-Afghani and has the most beautiful voice on the European jazz scene. Brighton loves jazz, and we have a big jazz Festival every other year."

We both lay on our backs on the rug, Owen blowing smoke rings, and totally absorbed in the music. I felt happy. After the concert we walked across the heath to The Spaniards Inn and I had my first Guinness, which I didn't like as was far too bitter, so Owen drunk it and bought me a pint of Pimm's instead.

"How's the library job going?" he asked me.

"I actually gave in my notice last week as I'm doing a lot of readings and need my energy."

"What do you charge for a reading?"

"Sixty pounds for an hour, or fifty pounds for forty-five minutes. Most people take the hour."

"So how many do you do in a week?"

"About four or five; it varies. I've also re-decorated my consulting room as it was getting a bit tired."

"Do you have any photos?"

Fortunately I did.

"It looks amazing. When are you going to do a reading for me, then?"

"I always have my cards with me, Owen. We could do a very simple three-card layout now, but I'll have to give you the interpretations later as a table in a pub garden isn't the right environment to do it in, and I feel a bit tipsy after the Cava and Pimms. It's never a good idea to mix alcohol with readings. Also I don't like to 'play' with the tools of my trade. Both the reader and the recipient have to respect the cards. They're not a party trick."

"Of course. That's fine."

Owen drew The Magician, followed by the Eight of Wands, and then the Nine of Pentacles.

"Interesting," I said. The Magician's a great card, and that is you, being as was the first card you drew. I'll give you a call with a more in-depth reading tomorrow."

"I look forward to that."

We walked to Hampstead tube, had our first kiss, and arranged to meet in Brighton the following Saturday.

On the train I couldn't resist checking the meaning of his cards in my handbag Tarot guide. They were good and favourable, and I made some notes. My feelings for Owen were developing, and I felt that we were comfortable and easy together, although he was much more cultured and intelligent than my previous boyfriends. I'm about as cultural as a can of tinned peaches, and also need to lose some weight before our first encounter. I texted him to thank him for the day, and suggested he call me the following evening to discuss the cards. My nagging doubt was with myself, that I'd lied to him, and was continuing to live the lie. This was wrong, but I seemed to be in it too deep and wasn't sure of the way out other than to be brutally honest with him, which may make him distrust me. My thoughts were diverted by a text from Elaine, asking if she could come for a reading in the morning, which was arranged. At least I didn't have to put on any airs with her. I gave her a five-card reading, and we looked up the meanings together. Her cards, all from the Minor Arcana, were fairly mediocre, suggesting that she was in a stale-mate, with decisions to be made, which she agreed with. People generally only seek consultations with a psychic if their situation need answers.

Owen called me that evening, and we went through his cards:

"The Magician is a card of strength, commitment and diplomacy," I told him. "This grounded man has the ability to make things happen, and can deal with life's negatives, but there are obstacles. It's also a card for new beginnings and success. The Eight of Wands is a free-flowing, positive and energetic card, suggesting travel and reachable goals. The arrows of love indicate a healthy relationship, with a clear sense of purpose, and room for both parties to have their own lives, but it's also a card for a protector and suggests family disorders and demands. The Nine of Pentacles is a good card if you're in the entertainment/communications business, suggesting a possible opportunity, and it assures financial independence and that material goals can be met with discipline and commitment."

"Wow," Owen said, "that's all so true. It's blown my mind. It's all very reassuring."

"The Magician and the Nine of Pentacles both suggest jealousy and difficulties, and the Eight of Wands can mean domestic responsibilities, which I guess has to do with your Mum," I told him, but all the cards allude to love and a good relationship. That sounds good for us. Yes?"

"Yes. And I'm really hoping you still want to come up to the Awards. Three of us are going up, but we're only staying at a Travelodge on the Friday night to keep expenses down. We could always go somewhere nicer for the Saturday night?"

"I don't mind. I'm not used to fancy hotels, but will you be able to get me a ticket for the ceremony?"

"Of course. Leave it to me, Candy."

I received a letter from the Library on Tuesday morning, saying that I wouldn't be paid for the month, and that in view of my unreliability they wouldn't be prepared to provide references for any future employment. Sod them, I thought, but I really did have to find another job as the small inheritance from my Nan wouldn't keep me going indefinitely. Over a latte in Pret's I had a brainwave, which was to approach 'Velvet Sunset' to see if they had any vacancies. I would surely meet some interesting people, and I felt empowered to go in and enquire right there and then.

"Good morning," I said to the guy at the till, who had dreadlocks down to his ankles and a dark complexion. "I'm Candy Jenkins, and am learning to become a Medium. I've bought loads of stuff from your shop, and would love to work here."

"You're an 'Answered Prayer', Candy," he said, "in the words of one of the Angel cards. I'm Jordan. My partner, Amber, owns the shop. One of our staff has recently had to give in her resignation for family reasons. She used to work on Tuesdays, Wednesdays and Thursdays. Could you do those days? The pay isn't massive at ten pounds an hour, but we love to have psychic people involved with the shop, and I'm sure it will bring you in some business. When could you start? Our hours are ten 'til five, and we're shut on Mondays."

"I could start immediately, but don't you need to take up references?" I asked him.

"No, I can tell from your aura that you're a genuine and trustable lady, so how about tomorrow? I can spend the day here with you and give you some basic training?"

"That sounds wonderful. Thanks so much, Jordan. Here's my mobile number and I'll see you tomorrow."

I couldn't believe my luck, and went to M&S to buy healthy salad lunches to take into work for Wednesday and Thursday, and a week's worth of their low-cal ready meals. I rang Angie to see if she wanted to meet for lunch, but she was busy, so I went to

H&M to buy some clothes for my new job. Whilst browsing, I got a call on my mobile, displaying 'number withheld' on the screen.

"Hi. Is that Psychic Candy?" a lady's voice, barely audible, asked me.

"Speaking."

"I understand you're a medium, and wondered if you do phone consultations? I got your number from someone who's close to me, so I'd rather not give my real name, if that's OK. Call me Sue."

I did some quick thinking and thought she could only have come through Elaine.

"That's fine, Sue. I only do Christian names anyway. To be honest, I'm just starting out, so we could do a five-card layout, using the camera on my phone for you to select your cards, then you'll have to call me later for my interpretations. I'm not charging at this stage, but maybe you could put a tenner in a charity box, if you thought it worthwhile."

"I'll do that. Could we do the reading now?" she asked.

"Sorry, Sue. I'm out shopping at the moment, but do call me again in a couple of hours and I'll be ready then. Let's say three o'clock, if that suits you."

"Thank you. Speak later then."

The word was clearly spreading, but phone consultations weren't something I'd been prepared for at this stage. I bought myself a fresh cream apple turnover from Greggs, which I ate on the bus. When I got home I changed into my psychic gear and got my room set up – lighting candles, joss-ticks, turning on the lava lamp and putting the Soft Pan Pipes on my CD player. Sue duly rang at three and I showed her myself with the camera, and gave her a quick virtual tour of the room. I then asked her to clear her mind and concentrate on the cards, while I shuffled them. For the first time they felt sticky, heavy and awkward. She selected her five cards from the middle pack, which I'd spread out in a fan. It seemed quite a good system, even though I was winging it. Her cards were a turbulent combination: Death reversed, The Hanged Man, Eight of Wands reversed, The Nine of Swords and The Four of Cups.

"I can tell you right away, Sue, that your life seems to be in turmoil, but let me analyse the cards in more depth, so if you can call me back at six, we can go through everything together." This was agreed on.

In a nutshell, her cards told me of fear, loneliness, inertia, lethargy, destroyed hopes and a lack of faith for the future. Also that her life was in suspension. Delays and unresolved obstacles were indicated, along with barriers and a lack of support, huge emotional burdens and self-blame.

I took a deep breath and went to make myself a cup of tea. I needed all of that time to analyse and study the cards' meanings and their interactions.

Sue rang back at on the dot of six and I went through each of the cards in detail, and of their relevance in a layout. I could hear her starting to cry.

"Sue, I don't know anything about you – where you live or what your real name is. I'm not here in any way to act as a counsellor, or to give you advice, but I think you need some professional help and guidance, if these are your true circumstances." I suddenly had a sharp sense of tapping into her silent aura.

"Your aura is making me see lilies, Sue. Not like lilies on a coffin, but I see you surrounded by them, and they're beautiful, but surreal. Are you a florist?" (Mediums are allowed to ask questions.) She blew her nose, and I continued:

"I'm also getting a rough sea and Indian temples with spires and domes. Maybe you're going on a cruise to India?"

"No. No cruise, and Indian temples don't have any significance either. I'm not a florist, but what you have seen with the lilies is true, although not in the way you think. I'm sorry, I'm going to hang up now, but thank you. Thank you so much."

I tried not to think too much about the worrying reading, or the poor woman, as it's not advisable to get personally involved with clients, but the chances were that I'd never hear from her again. The experience had a dampening effect on my expectant mood for the new job, so I took a long bath and ate two of the ready meals in my pyjamas, while binge-watching several episodes of Dinner Date.

I didn't sleep very well, but got myself up at eight on Wednesday and put on my new purple, pleated long skirt, a white T-shirt and a pink bandana. Jordan greeted me enthusiastically at the shop and made me a coffee.

"The week days tend to be quieter than at weekends, when Amber works. We get a lot of time-wasters, but you'll get used to that. Have you ever worked a till?" I admitted I hadn't, so he showed me how, and also how to do refunds. I wrote it all down. Some young girls came and bought various healing crystals.

"They're really popular now, but easily shopliftable," Jordan told me after they'd left. "We have CCTV, but it does happen." He showed me how to work the locks and the alarm. It was more responsibility than I'd ever had in a job. The day was rather long, with only three other customers, and I was tired by the time I got back home. Owen called me and I told him about my day.

"As it's Bank Holiday you can come up Saturday, Sunday or Monday this weekend. There's a Fun Weekend at Brighton

Pavilion, which I think you'll enjoy. It's in aid of The Down's Syndrome Association charity, which is one the radio station supports. There'll be live acts, food stalls, street entertainers and a steel band."

"You always have something interesting lined up, Owen. That sounds great. I'll come on Sunday as I'm going shopping with Angie on Saturday."

"Great. Look forward to seeing you then."

Thursday went well at the shop, and I enjoyed going through all the stock and looking at the different Tarot books. I mastered the till and sold a couple of Sita music CDs, some joss-ticks, and advised a lady about her choice of Tarot cards. I was starting to feel like an old hand in this game, and the karma of Velvet Sunset suited me ideally to study my own psychic and spiritual development. Although how long the shop could survive, with such little trade and low-cost items, was a worry. Angie came to collect me just before closing, and we went to The Blue Pineapple for cocktails to celebrate my new job, and then had a Chinese takeaway at hers. I told her about the mysterious woman and her terrible cards, and, as always, she advised me to be careful with dealing with strangers. I was much more 'devil-may-care' than her.

"And do you still think that Owen is who he says he is?" she asked me.

"Without a doubt. He's such a genuine guy. I'll introduce you when he next comes to Chelmsford."

"And have you – you know – yet?"

"No, but we're going up to Liverpool for some Awards ceremony in a few weeks time, and will spend the weekend together. Speaking of which, I'm meant to be on a diet! I'll re-start tomorrow."

I was really excited about the Fun Day, and wasn't disappointed. I'd never heard of The Brighton Pavilion before, and was totally gob-smacked. It looked like The Taj Mahal (which I only knew about from that famous photo of Princess Diana on the bench.) I suddenly had a feeling of deja-vu, with the Indian building I'd seen in my reading with Sue, but brushed it aside. We looked around the elaborate palace first.

"This was built in 1787 for George IVth as his seaside retreat, and was designed by John Nash," Owen told me. "Queen Victoria also had it for a while, but preferred to build her country home at Osborne House in The Isle of Wight. The Pavilion's quite the most funky and iconic architecture in Brighton, and we're very proud of it."

I wasn't really into history or dates, but the place had a great vibe. Everywhere we went, Owen was greeted enthusiastically.

"You seem to be very well known here, Owen," I said.

"It's only because of my job and the profile we give to this charity," he replied.

In the gardens we were entertained by a child-friendly Punch and Judy Show. (No clubbing each other to death with rolling pins), but still a string of sausages and a scary crocodile.

"I remember being delightfully terrified by Punch and Judy on Morecombe beach, where my grandparents lived then," I told Owen. "I think it's a shame now that things are now so P.C." Owen disagreed:

"You can't frighten children now, and especially those with special needs."

There was an old-fashioned Carousel, poetry recitals, gold-painted motionless human statues, cheerleaders, a yoga demonstration, and everything from candy floss to sushi and a pork hog roast on offer at the food stalls. We went for the hog roast in a bap, stuffed with pork crackling, apple sauce and mustard. It was to die for.

There were lots of children with Down's Syndrome there.

"God, those poor parents," I said. "Having a child with Down's must be so challenging. Do they live with their parents all their lives?"

"Not necessarily - it depends on the severity. There are different grades of the syndrome: some can go on to lead fairly normal and independent lives, and even get married, with arranged contraception of course. Now their life expectancy is about sixty years.

"You seem to know a lot about it," I said.

"That's because the radio station is very involved with mental health and community issues – ranging from Down's Syndrome to depression, anxiety, dementia, and of course domestic abuse. I think that Harry and Meghan are making great strides to raise awareness of all these issues, and I hold out great hopes for them. They're a great breath of fresh air, since Princess Diana."

"You're such a humane person, Owen." I said. "I've never given these things much thought."

He gave me a kiss.

"Now we're going to get some candy floss for Candy!"

I think that was the moment I started to fall in love with him.

He walked me back to the station and said that we couldn't meet up the following weekend as it was his Mum's birthday, and he was planning to take her away.

"How about Saturday 11th? I'd love to show you The Lanes."
"Where are you taking your Mum to?" I asked him.

"Err – to Eastbourne. She wants to see her Godmother, who's dying."

I felt sad not to see Owen for two weeks, but busied myself

in the shop. I studied books about 'aura readings' and how to get calibrated through meditation. I do find meditation difficult as it's meant to clear your mind, but all I can think about is what I'm having for lunch or supper, or what's in the fridge.

On Tuesday a middle-aged lady came in to the shop and I instantly felt a psychic connection with her. Most of our clientele are women. She was looking at the palmistry books.

"Excuse me," I said. "I've got a very strong psychic connection with you: I'm getting Swansea, and a baby called Anna or Anne. I'm also seeing piles of logs."

"Oh my God, this has freaked me out. I'm Pam, and you have a real gift. Could I come and see you for a reading? My son and daughter-in-law moved to Swansea six months ago. My daughter-in-law's tricky, and it didn't work out with them living with me in Chelmsford. Was a bit like Gavin and Stacey, so they moved out when Denise became pregnant, and I haven't heard from them since as my daughter-in-law said I was interfering. My granddaughter's called Annie-May, and my son's a forester."

At that moment I realised that I had a gift for reading a person's aura.

Pam had a good reading, and her cards showed me that things would be resolved, and family matters restored. Also – and most poignantly – that she was in for a big and unexpected surprise.

"The Star, your first card, signifies renewed hope and bright prospects." I told her. "It's a very positive card to end wasted effort and time. It brings power, energy, hope and faith. Your second card, Fortitude, represents power, energy and courage. It also promises success and honour. The other three cards from the Minor Arcana link in well to The Star and Fortitude. Do let me know if your reading has been productive, as I hold out great hopes."

"I will, Candy. Thank you so much. I'm going to recommend you to my friends."

It was time to start charging.

As the next weekend was free, I went to a day seminar at The Plantation Centre in Maldon on 'How to Tap into your Psychic Energy'. It was amazing, and I learnt a lot. Pam also referred me to her friend, who was pleased with her reading.

The following Saturday Owen met me at Brighton station, and we drove a few miles out of town to The Greenways Equestrian Centre.

"Oh my God, we're not going riding, are we? I'm not really dressed for it!" I said.

"No, Candy Floss, but there's someone I'd like you to meet."

We walked to the open enclosure and watched disabled children being led around the manege. As they approached where we were standing, a little girl – obviously with Down's Syndrome – called out "Dada, Dada!"

"Hi Lily. We've come to watch you have your riding lesson."

My mind shuffled about like a fruit machine, coming up with two lemons and an plum.

"Is this your daughter?" I asked him. "She's beautiful."

"Yes, this is Lily. She's eight. I wasn't exactly truthful with you, Candy. I don't live with my mother. I live with my wife and we share Lily's care, although our marriage is over, and has been for years. Things were very difficult after Lily was born, and my wife has a history of problems with anorexia and depression and isn't capable of looking after Lily on her own. This is all the truth, but now our relationship is developing I felt compelled to introduce you to Lily and put you in the real picture. I'm sorry I lied to you, but I thought you might be put off, as has happened in a previous relationship."

"Oh, Owen. Of course Lily hasn't put me off you." I felt quite emotional.

"I know this is all rather a lot for you to digest, Candy, but when Lily's finished her lesson we're going to go to MacDonalds, her favourite, if that's okay with you. She won't be up to understanding our relationship, but she will accept you right away as my friend, I promise."

"Tell me about Lily."

"She was our first, and only, child, and much anticipated after my wife had a miscarriage fairly late on in her first pregnancy. Julia had deep depression after losing the baby. I believe that stress can be linked with conception of a child with Down's Syndrome, but it's still being researched. It's a chromosomal irregularity, which can come from either parent, meaning that the baby will be born with an extra chromosome. We're still learning how to understand her. She needs routine and loves animals, music and Peppa Pig. She's incredibly affectionate, but can be stubborn. We think she understands far more than she can express, but fortunately there's a lot of help and support from The Down's Syndrome Association, and she goes to a special school. She has Trisomy 21 – the most common of the three types of Down's. Lily will always need care of some sort. That's it really. We just have to take it one day at a time."

I could see him holding back tears.

"I'm so sorry, Owen, it must put a terrible strain on your life. Thank you for telling me." He squeezed my hand, and we watched Lily for another twenty minutes or so, always waving happily every time she passed us.

Owen introduced us. "Lily, this is my friend: Candy. Candy, this is Lily."

"Candy floss! I love candy floss, Dada!" she beamed, as she hugged my thighs.

Lily was dark haired, with huge brown eyes and cherubic rosy cheeks. She was very demonstrative towards me, and insisted on holding my and Owen's hand as we walked from the car to MacDonalds. It all felt quite strange though, and had taken our relationship on to a new place. I quite forgave him for not telling me before about Lily, but still needed to come clean about my own lie. After Big Macs all round, Owen told me that his wife would shortly be coming to collect Lily.

"Would you rather we waited outside for her?" he asked thoughtfully.

"Of course not. I'd like to meet your wife, if that's alright with you."

I was shocked as this gaunt and incredibly thin woman approached our table. She had no expression in her sallow face and sunken eyes. Her hair was long and greasy, her clothes black and baggy. It was shocking, but I recognised her voice instantly. She was the woman who had called me and wanted to be known as Sue. Wow, this complicated things even further. Lily gave Owen and me a big hug.

"Dada will be back later, alright Lily? You be a good girl to Mummy."

We walked to a bar on the seafront and shared a bottle of rosé. I could have drunk the whole bottle myself in ten minutes. This had to be my moment.

"Owen. I've got something to tell you too, because I've also lied."

"Go on," he said. I took a deep breath.

"I'm not really a trained medium, as I told you. I didn't want to say I was a cleaner in the library, and a psychic medium seemed an intriguing alternative. It just came to me. Then I had to follow that lie. The amazing thing is that you've actually given me this new path in life, for which I can't thank you enough, as I think I'm developing a talent for it."

"That's fine, love", he laughed. "It's quite funny actually, so we're quits now. Yes?"

"Yes, but there's something else you need to know, which I've only just realised. A few weeks ago, I got a call from a lady, who didn't want to give her real identity as she told me that she had a close connection with someone who I knew. I said that was fine. I did a simple five card phone reading for her. Owen, her cards were horrendous: hopeless, with destroyed hopes, inertia, stagnation, self-blame and heavy responsibilities. But I really tapped into her aura and desperation. She was also surrounded by lilies. I also saw what I now realise was The Brighton Pavilion, but mistook it for a connection with India. There was a stormy sea too – rather like it is out there today. I probably shouldn't have done, but I recommended she get some professional help."

Owen swilled the wine around his glass, and lowered his head.

"Well, that's interesting, because I think she must have taken your advice. She went to the doctor a few weeks back, having refused to do so for ages, and she's been put on anti-depressants and has also agreed to attend a weight clinic, which is real progress. I guess she must have gone through my phone contacts, as she's done that before. I had you under 'Psychic Candy'. I expect she thought you were a contact for the radio station. I've made it quite clear to Julia that our marriage is over, but how can I leave her in the state she's in? She's not capable of work and is very reliant on me. We don't have the money to live separately anyway, and she wouldn't be capable of looking after Lily on her own."

"Yes, I can see that. I'm so sorry."

Owen took my hand. You can see that a relationship with me has its disadvantages, so if you want out, I'll quite understand."

"Of course I don't want out, Owen. I'm not like that. We were destined to meet, by some Higher Power."

I don't think that either of us could think of anything more to say on the subject, as there was so much to take in.

"So, you didn't take your Mum to Eastbourne then?" I asked him.

"No. We took Lily to Peppa Pig World. It's not too far from here, and we made a weekend of it. She was in seventh heaven. Sorry, that's another thing I lied about. Oh dear, I'm sorry, Candy. I'm not in the habit of telling lies, I promise you. God, that sounds like a lie too. Shit. Let's forget all this and discuss the arrangements for the Awards next Friday: I'm going up on the train with our P.R. Director and Audio and Digital Manager. Trains go from Euston and take around two and a half to three hours. We're planning to get there mid-afternoon, chill out a bit at the Travelodge, and get changed to be at the Cathedral for around six. It's black tie. Then there will be a Reception for all the nominees, followed by dinner at seven, and the ceremony starts at eight-thirty. I suggest you aim to arrive around the same time as us. I've told Tracey and Anthony that you're coming, and you needn't worry – they're lovely people. You'll really like them.

"I'm really looking forward to it, Owen, but it's a shame it's being held in Liverpool and not a more interesting location like Oxford or Edinburgh."

"Don't worry. I thought we'd hire a car on Saturday morning and drive down to Chester, where I've booked us in to Frogg Manor for the night. It's the most beautiful eighteenth century manor house - Google it."

"I can't wait, Owen. I really can't."

We walked to the station, hand in hand, and I felt truly happy with my life and with so much to look forward to.

I was thinking about my outfit as I travelled up to Liverpool on Friday, and hoped it would be okay. It was a long, maroon, sleeveless velvet dress with a plunging 'V' neckline, decorated with diamonte, and had cost me an arm and a leg at Debenhams. I'd only worn it once Angie's thirtieth birthday in Smiths seafood Restaurant in Ongar last year. I also took my grandmother's lace shawl, some black stiletto's and a matching clutch bag. But I did invest in some new, sexy, underwear from Ann Summers and a new faux-silk, pearl-coloured dressing gown.

Owen and his colleagues were having a bottle of champagne in the bar when I arrived. Introductions were made and their mood was high. After a second bottle was opened, I went upstairs to have a leisurely bath and get ready. Owen came up when I was doing my make-up and changed into his dinner jacket and a harlequin-patterned waistcoat. The Cathedral was an awesome building: Neo-Gothic with amazingly high stone arches and huge stained-glass windows. It was buzzing with the hundred and twenty-four nominees, their partners and colleagues, including Lenny Henry and several celebrities from the casts of Hollyoaks, Emmerdale and Coronation Street. I was quite overawed, drank far too much Prosecco, and only picked at my food over dinner. By the time the ceremony started I was starting to feel a bit whoozy, so stopped drinking.

The lights dimmed just before eight-thirty, and the sound of birdsong came through the sound system for a few minutes. It had a very unexpected, calming and reflective effect. Then a spotlight slowly illuminated the Compère on the stage.

"Ladies and Gentleman, thank you all so much for coming along this evening. Without you these prestigious annual Awards wouldn't happen. Each and every one of our Nominees here deserve to be recognised for outstanding achievements and commitment to making our world a better place. In this beautiful and serene setting of Liverpool's Cathedral, may I introduce your Hosts for tonight's National Diversity Awards: No less than the beautiful, talented and unique female vocalist for the Scissor Sisters: Ana Matronic, and from Big Brother to Ultimate Big Brother to Hell's Kitchen, and now a famous television Presenter: I give you Brian Dowling."

The hosts were given a standing ovation.

It all became rather a blur after the Awards for Entrepreneur of Excellence, Celebrity of the Year, and Diverse Company and Lifetime Achiever, and goodness knows what else. The clapping was endless. Eventually the hosts got to our category for the Award for Community Organisation and Multi-Strand. (I wasn't sure what that meant.) Owen gave me a nudge and topped up my glass. Brian Dowling cleared his throat:

"This Award – most deservedly – goes to a non-profit-making organisation, which reaches out to all sections of its community. Focusing on everything from racial and mental health issues through to developing the musical, cultural, religious and charitable aspects of its audience. Their vibrant mix is indeed multi-stranded in every way, supporting and representing the community of Brighton and Hove. Ladies and Gentlemen, it gives me the greatest of pleasure to present this coveted Award to

Radio Reverb." Everyone clapped, while Tracey went up to collect the Trophy. As she was walking back to our table the applause subsided and I clearly saw a vision of her becoming levitated and surrounded by a glowing light. It was unnerving, but I brushed the apparition aside.

When the ceremony had finished everyone slowly filtered out of the Cathedral, and Owen had a smoke. He, Tracey and Anthony wanted to go to a bar to celebrate, but I felt exhausted and had actually had enough. Everything had overwhelmed me and left me feeling ignorant and sorry for myself.

"Owen, could I have a word?" I interrupted him.

"Yes, love. Give us a kiss. Wasn't it fantastic? Are you okay? You look a bit unsteady."

"I'm fine, and am so happy and proud of you all, but I've a thumping headache and felt rather claustrophobic in there. Would you mind if I went back to the hotel and skipped the drinks?"

"Of course not. We'll grab a taxi and drop you off. I won't be late."

I felt I had let myself, but more importantly Owen, down. Why did I always have to fuck things up? I always screw up relationships. Dan was fun and the sex great, but he was a mechanic and all he wanted to talk about was Formula 1 and go racing in his banger. It became boring (and muddy), but now – at the other end of the scale – I feel intimidated by Owen and his colleagues' social awareness and intelligence. I fit in nowhere. I took a Diazepan and went to bed, but I'd not brought my nightie, so felt cold and put my jersey on. I was awake when Owen returned just after midnight, but pretended to be asleep. He kissed me on my forehead and slipped in to bed in his boxer shorts.

I woke at nine on Sunday and made us a cup of tea from the complimentary bedroom tray, although the kettle was very furred up and no bigger than a small milk bottle. At least I'd remembered to bring my new dressing gown. Owen was fast asleep, so I took a shower and dressed. It all seemed to be a most unfortunate start for our weekend away, and I felt it was all my fault.

"Owen, I've made you a cup of tea. It's getting cold." He groaned and rolled over.

"Hangover from Hell. Paracetamols in my sponge bag."

I got them and sat down on his side of the bed.

"I'm sorry about last night, Owen. It was very selfish of me not to join you to celebrate after your success with the Award. I was just a bit overcome by everything and felt out of my depth. I hope I didn't let you down or embarrass you." He sat up.

"It really doesn't matter, Candy. Don't beat yourself up. We were just on such a high and I got lost in all that. I'll get dressed and we'll go down for breakfast. Full English is what we both need."

Tracey and Anthony had nearly finished their breakfasts by the time we got down. I went for the continental buffet, but Owen needed the full Monty. I think we all had hangovers. The others had to get back, so we went upstairs to pack and Owen ordered our hire car.

Once out of Liverpool, we drove through rolling green countryside. Frogg Manor was the most beautiful place I'd ever stayed in. We were given The Wellington Room, which had a draped, canopied bed, an enormous chandelier and chintz furnishings.

"My God, Candy, look at this: we've even got a vintage radio, and it works! So cool."

We skipped lunch and went for a long walk.

"I didn't say so last night, Candy, but you looked gorgeous. Let's head back to the hotel as there's some unfinished business! For some reason I always feel horny when I've got a hangover – it must be some basic survival instinct - but I haven't showered today, so let's have a bath first."

I ran the slipper bath, tipped in the Jo Malone bubble sachets, and put on my new black undies.

"Wow! I've only been faithful to myself for the past three years, Candy, so you may need to be forgiving on the performance front. You're so well-covered and sexy. Julia used to be like that." This strange compliment couldn't have been more off-putting, but that's men for you. I was already in the wrong mind-set. After he'd soaped me and was clearly ready for action, we went to our sumptuous four-poster bed. It didn't take long, and I faked it. Then Owen fell asleep, so I consulted my Angel cards for a one-card answer. I drew 'Harmony', which reassured me that conflict was resolved in a situation which was troubling me. 'Know that you deserve this peace and happiness, and accept it graciously' was the message on the card. This put everything into perspective.

The best part of the day was dinner in the candle-lit dining room. Whilst consulting our menus in the Lounge, Owen ordered a bottle of champagne, followed by a bottle of red. We both chose from the set dishes of the day - local scallops and bacon salad, followed by roast duck, and then treacle tart with clotted cream. It was an amazing meal, and apart from the rather unsatisfactory physical business, a lovely stay at Frogg Manor.

When we were on the train going back to London, I got a call from Pam, the lady I'd had a strong psychic connection to in the shop a few weeks earlier and done a reading for. She told me with great excitement that the surprise I'd predicted had come true and she was to be awarded an M.B.E. for her years of voluntary work for the homeless in Chelmsford.

"That's fantastic, Pam. Many congratulations. You really deserve it. I'm so happy for you. Do keep in touch."

"Who was that?" Owen asked.

"One of my clients, who I foresaw being rewarded for her voluntary work in a local drop-in centre for the homeless over the past twenty-five years. She's going to get an M.B.E."

"Wow. You're getting good at this game, Candy."

I told him about the vision I'd had of Tracey in the Cathedral. "I hope it's nothing, Owen, but it was so vivid. You won't say anything to her, will you?"

"No, of course not, but what do you think it meant?" I didn't answer his question.

"Speaking of my visions, I would really like to do some general predictions on your station with my Tarot cards. That is if you still think it's a good idea."

"Very few of our programmes are pre-recorded and those that are, are usually put in the slot when someone lets us down. We feel it's more real if broadcasted live, so you would be talking live on air and that could be intimidating, but I'll discuss it with the team and see if we can find you a half-hour slot if they're agreeable. We've never done anything like this before, but there's certainly a mystic audience in Brighton. You feel confident enough to do it, then?"

"Yes, but the questions would all have to be of a non-personal nature – possibly predictions on general matters."

"I think that would be great. I'll see what I can do, love."

We said goodbye at Euston and went our separate ways, agreeing to meet in Chelmsford the following weekend. Owen said he'd like to meet Pam and visit the drop-in Centre to see how it compares with their one in Brighton.

"I'll ask her. I'm sure that will be fine. Bye for now, then Owen, and thank you for a wonderful time."

The idea of the Tarot broadcast seemed to go down well, and I found myself on the train down to Brighton the following Thursday, there having been a cancellation for a half-hour slot at two o'clock. I rang Jordan to say I couldn't go in to work, and he was very excited for me. On arrival at Radio Reverb I was greeted by Owen and then briefed by Anthony: "Your slot has been advertised on air this morning, and we have requested questions on global issues. The four most suitable ones will be chosen, but you won't be advised of them beforehand. After you've been introduced by Geoffrey, our Presenter, if you could spend a few moments saying a little bit about yourself and that it's your first 'radio reading', then I will ask you the first question. There will be a clock in the studio, so please try to stick to about three minutes for each answer. Owen will be with you. We'll have a little trial run in our second studio now. If you could try to speak slower than you normally would, and not to sound too monosyllabic. When the light goes out in the studio, the broadcast is finished."

That having gone well, Owen and I went out to a sandwich bar for a quick bite, and at quarter to two I was taken into the main recording studio, where a baize table was set up. I was fitted with a microphone and headset. The two technicians behind the glass screen gave me the thumbs up, and Owen poured me a glass of water. I gripped my cards as the timer went down to zero and Geoffrey, the presenter, came through my headphones. I hoped that my thumping heart couldn't be heard on air.

"A very good afternoon to all our listeners. As you may have heard earlier today, our advertised programme has been changed, but – and who could have foreseen this? We're very lucky to have Candy Jenkins with us instead. Candy's a psychic medium from Essex, and is going to consult her Tarot cards for answers to pre-selected questions from our public on general issues. I can see her shuffling the cards now, and splitting the pack in to three. Here she is, and she has no idea what the questions will be." Owen nodded at me.

"Hi everyone. I'm Candy. It's a great pleasure for me to be here with you today – even though I didn't predict it! Doing a live reading on air is a first for me, but I'm ready to give it a go. For those who aren't familiar with the Tarot, my cards give answers, but I also get guidance and images from my own visions. I'm sure there will be disbelievers out there, but my cards don't lie." I nodded at Anthony.

"Thank you, Candy, and welcome to Radio Reverb. Your first question: 'What is the future of our Royal Family?'"

"This is a big question, and a big family, Geoffrey, so I'm going to select four cards from my central pile. My first card, The Three of Swords, indicates despair, heartbreak, loss and betrayal. I'm getting Edward and Wallis Simpson, and also damage to the reputation of the royal household, with potential separation. My second card, The Five of Swords, suggests family rows and disharmony, resulting in scandal. I feel that this might be to do with Princes William, Harry and Meghan. We now have The Ten of Cups, but it's upside down (known as reversed), again suggesting problems, upheaval and relocation. My final card for this question is The Queen of Hearts. In this layout it indicates bitterness, heartbreak, and the betrayal of a child, causing grief and bitterness. I'm seeing ships and naval badges, which suggests it might be something to do with Prince Andrew. So, this spread shows a change afoot, and disruption within our Monarchy. I'm going to re-shuffle my cards again now, in preparation for Geoffrey's next question.

"Well, a lot to take in there, folks. My next question for Candy is 'What are your predictions for world famine and health?'"

"My first card is The Tower – a strong card from the Major Arcana. It can be positive, but needs another one to be drawn to give me a better picture. Ah, I've got The Ten of Swords. The suit of Swords normally indicates health issues and hidden enemies. This combination suggests a breakdown of established structures, and speaks to me of plague and sickness on a worldwide scale. There will always be famine, but something is worrying me more on a global scale – death, disruption, and an unforeseen deconstruction of the world as we know it."

"Strong words, Candy. Maybe we're in for a plague, like the Spanish Flu in 1918. Around a hundred years before that it was the French Revolution, so maybe these 'cullings' take on hundred-year cycles. This is worrying, but now on to your next question: 'What does the future hold for world affairs and wars?'"

"Thank you, Geoffrey. I'm going to go for a one-card answer, and I've drawn the Death card, but don't panic! This card relates to re-births and transformations, and doesn't always indicate death, but in this instance, it's showing me change and new beginnings. We all have Brexit on our minds, and I feel that it will go ahead and that we will become an independent island again, albeit with profound resistance and upheaval. I'm also getting The White House and political change there, resulting in lies, riots and dissent. But old patterns will be destroyed, revealing a new and rewarding path. Death is always a transitional cycle card."

"Well, watch this space. We're now on to our final question

for Candy, which is on the subject of the future of global and climate issues."

"I've split my pack into three, and am going to select three cards from the middle pile. Most appropriately, my first card is The World, which again suggests the changing cycles of our planet Earth. It's a card of reaping what you sow, and of synchronising to the rhythms of our environment. My second card, The Page of Cups, shows me a young, pioneering woman, with a loving heart and in tune with nature. She will usher in fresh energy and insights into saving the destruction of our world. I'm seeing Hansel and Gretal's gingerbread cottage, and thinking that her name may be Gretal, or something similar, and of Scandinavian origin. This girl will inspire the world with her passion about how we are destroying our planet, and she will be rewarded for her inspirational efforts – particularly in relation to raising awareness of plastic contamination of our oceans and sea life. My final card is The Wheel of Fortune. These three cards – all from the Major Arcana – shed light on our planetary failings, suggesting that there are new, innovative ways to sow seeds for the preservation of our future. The Wheel of Fortune tells us that what goes around comes round again. I see a reduction in carbon emissions, less consumption of meat, and moving towards electric cars as standard, and also raising awareness to live a more organic lifestyle. As far as climate change is concerned, I'm getting Noah's Ark and more regular flooding. But the cards really do indicate that as a human race we are now becoming aware of what we need to do to preserve and save our beautiful world. I think this is a powerful and positive note to end my reading on. Thank you very much."

"Thank you, Candy. This has been a fascinating and insightful experience. May I ask you what sort of timescale your predictions are?"

"I would say up to the next three years, but obviously indefinitely for global and climate issues."

"Sadly, Candy doesn't live locally, but she does telephone readings and can be contacted through us." The light in the studio went out and the guys behind the screen gave me the thumbs up again.

Geoffrey continued: "Now, back to our advertised schedule, I'm delighted to welcome Ruben Hein to take us through his choices for Thursday afternoon's Relax with Jazz Hour."

Owen gave me a hug. "Candy, that was amazing. You're a natural. Did you feel nervous? You certainly didn't sound it."

"I was really nervous at the beginning, but then the cards showed me the way and I moved in to a different gear."

"Impressive. It'll be interesting to see what feedback we get – and hopefully some telephone bookings for you too. I've got a meeting in forty-five minutes, so I'll order you a taxi back to the station, but come and say goodbye to Geoffrey and Anthony first."

Without sounding big-headed, I was proud of my achievement, and felt that my life was taking on a new direction. My three-card layout on the train back home suggested opportunities and positive change. I fancied a rewarding double white-hot chocolate from Pret's, and popped in to Velvet Sunset as the shop was still open. Jordan was reading and looked pale.

"Candy, how did it go today? You haven't missed much here. It's been very quiet and I've got a stinking cold. Would you mind coming in tomorrow instead of today? I'm open late because a lady made a big order on-line, but said she could only come in at six. It's now half-past, but she hasn't turned up."

"Of course not. Today went really well, thank you. Why don't you go home now, and I'll shut up the shop and wait a bit longer."

"Great, thanks. Do let me know if she comes. Her order's in this box and is nearly a hundred quid of stuff, but it's all paid for."

Owen called me as I was eating the fish and chips I'd picked up on the way home.

"Love. Hope you got back safely? I've got some great news for both of us: we've had fourteen calls requesting your contact details for a telephone reading. Also I've just had a meeting with Ruben Hein, a contemporary Dutch musician, who was on air after you. He's offered me a job with Jazz Maastricht as their travelling sound technician when they tour. They go all over the world, although the work would be irregular, but well paid. It would mean I would have to give up my permanent job here, but perhaps work part-time. What do you think?"

"Wow. Congratulations. Are you going to go for it?"

"Well, it rather depends on Julia, but she's been going to her weight clinic and taking a bit more trouble with her appearance. My mother can always help out with Lily, and the job won't start until next Spring, so I'm going to go for it."

"Fantastic, Owen. It's been a great day for both of us, but I'm tired, and now working at the shop tomorrow. So shall I meet you at Chelmsford station around midday on Saturday? Perhaps we can visit Pam at the Homeless Centre and help them serve up lunch? And if you could spare a night, I'll book us in somewhere nice."

"Cool. See you then. What a week it has been for us both, Candy, but I've got to sort out Lily and get her to bed now. Love you."

On Friday morning I was surprised to see Jordan and Amber come into the shop.

"Thanks for covering today, Candy." Jordan said. "A pain that that that woman didn't collect her order yesterday, but sorry to keep you in late. To be honest, we're struggling here and want to sell the business. Would you like to take it on?"

Opportunities came to mind, and I thought fast and clearly.

"Golly. I do think that this sort of shop is a matter of venue. As I've just had such a positive experience and response to my radio reading in Brighton, I may buy your stock and relocate there." Jordan and Amber exchanged looks.

"I'll need to do some spade-work though. What would the shop stock be priced at?"

"About four thousand pounds", Amber replied.

"Let me give it some thought guys, but it's a really interesting proposition."

I missed Owen and was pleased he was coming to Chelmsford tomorrow as I'd so much to discuss with him. He'd arranged for his mother to stay over and help look after Lily. I'd booked us in to The Blue Boar in Maldon, a fourteenth century coaching inn, for the Saturday night so as to avoid his cat allergy. He'd like the character and history of the place. I spent most of the day going through all the stock in the shop and itemising it and reckoned I could make do with smaller premises. It was very exciting.

Owen and I met at the railway station on Saturday and took a cab to The Sanctus Homeless Centre, which is near where I live. We met Pam and helped to dish out shepherd's pie, and were invited to stay for lunch. Their cafe was bright and cheerful. I'd no idea how many homeless people there were in Chelmsford. Pam said that Chelmsford, Harlow and Southend were the worst affected towns in Essex. We helped wash up and then walked back to my house.

Angie very kindly collected us and drove us to Maldon. She was curious to meet Owen, and it seemed like a good opportunity. I hadn't told him where we were going, as was to be a surprise and my treat.

We had a few beers in the beamed bar and then Angie left and we walked down the old-fashioned high street to the quay, where Owen was interested in the many moored Thames barges.

"This is a lovely town, Candy, but look at all that mud!"

"I know. They have an annual mud race in August – people dress up in Viking gear and fund-raise. It's a great spectacle. Angie and I came to watch last year."

"I'd like to do that," Owen said.

We walked, hand in hand, to the end of the Promenade, taking in an ice cream on the way, and sat in the shelter. I couldn't wait any longer to tell Owen about the possibility of buying Velvet Sunset's stock.

"I've been giving this so much thought, Owen, but there's no point in staying in their premises in Chelmsford. So, I've had a crazy thought of renting out my house and renting shop premises in Brighton. I've already got six telephone readings, booked for next week from your radio audience. It just seems like I'm meant to be down there to continue my new life. Ideally I'd lease a shop, with rooms above, for a year to give it a good go. My cards have told me that there are opportunities to be taken. Plus, I would be nearer to you. What do you think?"

"I think it's a fabulous idea, love. Very exciting. Let's get back to the Blue Boar and check out retail units on the net. There are so many little shops in The Lanes, and I'm sure a lot of them would have upstairs accommodation."

"So I wouldn't be invading your space, then?" I asked him.

"Not at all. We're good together, Candy, and have been

together now for nearly two months, while taking things steadily. I love your company, and you've been so understanding about Lily and my circumstances."

Owen ordered a bottle of Prosecco in the timbered bar and got out his lap top. There were masses of shops to let, but not many with upstairs residential space. I particularly fell in love with an arch on the West Pier at £7,850 per annum. It could just about be affordable if I did readings there, and in the evenings.

"I'm sure something will come up for you, Candy, as it always does. But... roll the drums: it's a bit of a double celebration because I've formally accepted the job at Maastricht Jazz and will get my contract next week. They mostly travel to festivals in Europe during the summer, but further afield in the winter months, like to The States and Australia. Chicago and New York are great cities for jazz, and I can still keep my job at Radio Reverb, albeit slightly reduced. Most of the festivals are over weekends, when I don't work anyway. So, shall we toast to our new futures then, Candy?" We clinked glasses.

"Cheers, Owen. Here's to our futures, then. And not forgetting the cucumber text!"

ACKNOWLEDGEMENTS

I would like to thank Bunny Farnell-Watson, Faye Harrison, Caroline and Robin Lodge, Kay MacCauley, Connie Menting, Poppy Razzell (for her beautiful handwriting for *The Birds and the Bees*), Lee Sharp, Alexander Skeaping, and the endlessly patient Katie Isbester at Clapham Publishing for their help and support.

Also, the lovely team at Radio Reverb, and the family of the late Tracey Allen.

Finally, my grateful thanks to St Technos*, my personal Greek God of Technology, for being on my side – most of the time.

*Technology – Wikipedia

Technology ("science of craft", from Greek τέχνη, techne, "art, skill, cunning of hand"; and -λογια, -logia) is the sum of techniques, skills, methods, and processes used in the production of goods or services or in the accomplishment of objectives, such as scientific investigation.

Etymology. The word technology comes from two Greek words, transliterated techne and logos. Techne means art, skill, craft, or the way, manner or means by which a thing is gained. Logos means word, the utterance by which inward thought is expressed, a saying, or an expression.

ABOUT THE AUTHOR

Nettie Firman is an artist and lives in Essex.

This is her second collection of short stories. Her first book, *Crickets on Cocaine*, was published in 2020.

"Her attention to the detail of attraction is formidable and reads true."

Francis Gerard

"This debut collection of short stories delivers the reader into the seemingly normal lives of its characters. However, all is not as it seems. Their lives are interjected with drama, and we see the true face of human nature appear. Utterly gripping: you will devour each story and be left wanting to know more about the lives you have just witnessed."

Adrian Hill

"Sharply incisive observations of characters, and the stark unspoken thread of darkness."

Cathy Clarke

.

Lightning Source UK Ltd.
Milton Keynes UK
UKHW011028140821
388796UK00002B/90